Dream Cottage

Harriet J Kent

Clink
Street

London | New York

Published by Clink Street Publishing 2015

ISBN: 978-1-909477-79-7
Ebook: 978-1-909477-80-3

Chapter One

"Do you, Maxim Cosmo Berkley, take Greta Olivia Standing to be your lawful wedded wife? Will you promise to love, to honour and to cherish her?"

The packed hotel suite in Cowes on the Isle of Wight lay silent as the guests awaited Max's response. A distant throat clearing and pathetic dry cough broke the silence.

Max drew a short intake of breath and closed his eyes before breaking into a large grin. He turned to the congregation, opened his eyes and yelled.

"Yes! I bloody well *will!*"

The room exploded into spontaneous cackles of laughter and chaotic cheering as the minister calmly regained control of the ceremony. Patting the air to cease the over-excited throng, she cleared her throat. She tried to make light of Max's overenthusiastic response.

"I think you've made yourself *quite* clear, Maxim. Now, do you, Greta Olivia Standing, take Maxim Cosmo Berkley as your lawful wedded husband? Will you promise to love, to honour and to cherish him, so long as you both shall live?"

Greta wasn't paying attention. She was looking down at the floor. She had noticed a large, fleshy black spider flashing across the dark red patterned carpet. It disappeared momentarily into the brown and black swirls of the carpet's weave. It reappeared, camouflaged in places, but clearly on a mission. Greta froze in horror as it nonchalantly made its way towards the hem of her delicately trimmed, off the shoulder, ivory wedding dress. She looked on in sheer terror as the spider commenced its awkward ascent of her embroidered satin train. Greta found herself in a stifled panic. She opened and closed her mouth, gasping for breath. Her face was beginning to blush; she felt hot, she felt nauseous. She looked in horror, openmouthed at the minister, who gently, but persuasively, prompted a reply. She began to flap her arms rapidly. Her sweet-smelling rose bouquet shred pretty pink petals that cascaded gracefully to the floor around Greta's feet.

"Greta? Would you care to respond to your vows?"

Greta tried to regain her composure as the spider edged further up her dress. It was now at thigh height.

"Er. Um. Can you *please* help me?" she looked desperately at the minister. "I'm really sorry but I can't say anything until someone gets rid of *that*!" she screamed and pointed to her dress and closed her eyes. She let out a shrill, blood-curdling shriek at the top of her voice. She couldn't breathe; she felt paralysis seeping through her body, like an intoxicating suffocation by an invisible hand. The guests were speechless; the room was still. From their seated point in the congregation, it appeared as though Greta was pointing directly at Max. The guests looked at each other in bewilderment. They weren't sure whether this was one of Max's pranks, which had somehow imploded on its delivery.

"What *is* the matter, Greta?" the minister asked impatiently.

"Just get rid of it! Get it off my dress! I suffer with arachnophobia and there is one of… urgh… them on my dress!" she screamed. "I can't even bear to say what it is! Urgh!" Greta was awkwardly stepping from side to side, flapping her bouquet in an attempt to swat at the spider.

Max looked around the fabric of the wedding dress and found the rather plump spider balancing awkwardly on the side of Greta's hip. He flicked it with his hand and it spiralled across the room on to the floor. Greta continued to scream in despair.

"You idiot! Why didn't you use a piece of paper and a glass to capture it? Now I don't know where it is! It could be anywhere. Find it, Max; do something!"

"It's probably dead," surmised Max. "It took the full force of my hand. Either that or it is winded. Unfortunately I don't have a piece of paper *or* a glass with me at this present moment in time. Look, darling, can we just carry on and get married?"

"Not until I know where it is. You know how I can't even bear to look at one of those disgusting things! Just do it, Max, or you'll ruin my day!" Greta snivelled. She patted at her cheeks, which were reaching boiling point. She suddenly felt faint. She looked wildly around her, much to the amusement of the guests. The minister restored what order she could as idle chatter began to filter through the room.

"Ladies and gentlemen. We will resume the ceremony shortly. If you could please remain seated. Thank you for your understanding in this... er... interruption." She smiled warmly at them and then turned to Greta and glared.

"We *are* short on time; I do have another ceremony to officiate at in half an hour. I fully understand your predicament. Admittedly, I don't like spiders either, but I am damn sure one wouldn't ruin my wedding ceremony. We can't spend ages looking for it. Just compose yourself Greta, please!"

"Sorry, but if you don't find that... that thing, I am walking out of here, right now!" Greta snapped. Her face was inches away from the minister's. Her lips were pursed so tightly that her designer peony stain lipstick was invisible. Her eyes were screwed up in tight defiance. Her neck was elegantly long and swanlike but her veins were visibly protruding like pulsating tendrils, with meaningfulness, tinged with fear.

Max, along with his best man, Fabian, who had been urged by Max with a thump from his elbow to start a search party, desperately scoured the carpet and wooden floor boundary to find the offending arachnid.

"For pity's sake, it's only a spider!" Fab complained bitterly, as he crawled along the floor in his morning suit. His cravat was fastened so tightly, he could hardly move his neck; he felt breathless and restricted. He sighed as he made his way through lines of sandaled feet, selectively painted toenails and freshly polished leather brogues. He apologised as he scanned all areas of the floor. A surprising number of female guests sniggered and squealed as they strategically parted their legs to enable Fab a clear passage. Fab blinked and shook his head in amazement as an array of rather inappropriate panties, stocking tops and hemlines flashed before him.

"You know what she's like; hates anything that has more than four legs," Max returned as he wrestled with a pair of varicose-veined calves. "Sorry, I do apologise..." he uttered time and time again.

"And she's desperate to live in the countryside? She won't last there long; the place is full of spiders! Ah, here it is!" Fab picked up a black mass of entangled legs. The spider he had discovered had clearly been deceased for more than a few minutes; probably a few days.

"Are you quite sure that's it?" Max didn't look convinced.

"Course I'm not; but it will do. She'll buy it; you know how gullible she is!" Fab smiled and rose to his feet. Holding the dead spider high above his head so all could view it, he straightened his jacket, adjusted his silk cravat and ran a hand swiftly through his mass of black swept-back hair. A small flurry of applause erupted from the back of the room.

"Okay everyone! I have found it! The spider is dead!" he announced in his thick Italian accent in animated triumph. "The wedding ceremony can now continue!"

Greta looked suspiciously at Fab as he resumed his position alongside Max.

"Keep it well away from me, do you hear?" she ordered and turned to face the minister. "Right, can we start please? From the beginning as I have lost the ambience of the occasion."

"I am very short on time, Greta. So if you can just say '*I do*', I will carry on from there." The minister forced a gritted smile.

"No way! I can't remember what you said before. The urgh… spider, urgh, put me off!" She rearranged her dress and rechecked for the offending animal. "Urgh, it was so horrible!"

The minister sighed and hurriedly repeated the vows. Greta concentrated hard and then, to everyone's relief, cleared her throat and said in a crystal clear voice,

"I do."

A cheer erupted from the congregation in relief as the minister confirmed, "You are now husband and wife; congratulations! Maxim, you may kiss your bride!"

Greta still felt very faint and her breathing was shallow.

As Max leant forward to plant a kiss on Greta's lips, to his disbelief he saw the spider, far from demised, triumphantly resting on the back of Greta's elegant diamante tiara. He could clearly see its legs, which were a marginally lighter shade of brown than Greta's hair, against her ivory coloured veil. He closed his eyes and quickly pecked Greta on the lips as though he had been burnt. Greta glared at him.

"Was that it?" she asked, clearly disappointed.

"Yep, for now, my beautiful wife. Come on, let's get out of here!" Max grabbed Greta by the hand, bypassing the photographer who was trying to get some ad lib shots of the happy couple, and rushed outside towards the neighbouring car park.

"What *is* the matter with you?" Greta stopped him in the doorway of the hotel. "We have to sign the register." She was confused over her husband's strange and totally out of character antics. Cool, calm Max was acting like a man possessed.

"Allow me to do one thing for you; before we go back in," Max tried to stay calm.

"Okay. What?"

"Close your eyes, stay still and all will be revealed," Max was focussed on the position of the spider as it clambered to get a better grip of the tiara. "Do as I say!" His voice had an authority which Greta found strangely attractive. Her heart fluttered in anticipation. He focused on the spider. With his feet apart, he made his move.

"Okay; I'm waiting," she closed her eyes and remained statuesque.

In an instance, Max thrust his hand at Greta's tiara and ripped it harshly from her hair. He tossed it to the ground and stamped on it.

"What the hell are you doing?" she gasped. "You really pulled my hair! What's this all about? Are you deliberately trying to ruin my day and my hairdo?"

Max continued to stamp on the tiara until it was an unrecognisable mashed up mass of metal with its sparkling diamante stones amassed on the ground. He saw the spider; it hadn't survived the ordeal; it was well and truly dead. Max picked up the tiara, reshaped it, brushed it off and handed back to Greta, who stood open-mouthed at his outburst.

"What *was* all that about? Are you completely mad?" she was dumbfounded.

"That, my dear, was the traditional ritual of all Berkley menfolk when they marry," Max blagged, straight-faced and with pure perfection. "For as long as I can remember, both my father and grandfather had always said that all Berkley men would remove the headdress from their newly wedded wife's hair, throw it to the floor and crush it. It is a sign, as it was of my forefathers', of my lifelong commitment to you." He drew Greta close to him and kissed her lustfully on her cheek. "Trust me!" he whispered. "You will always remember this moment; believe me, you'll love me forever for it!"

He took a glance at the spider; it was now an unrecognisable wet splodge on the tarmac.

"Forgive me father, for I have sinned," he whispered beneath his breath and ushered Greta back inside the hotel to sign the register.

□□□

Greta was overcome and not quite sure of all the strange happenings of the past few minutes. She tottered back to the hotel suite. The minister had positioned the register on a table festooned with two artificial posies of rather dusty looking lilies and orchids. Greta turned her nose up distastefully as they didn't blend in with her own colour scheme. She casually pushed them aside and placed her own bouquet on the table. She checked her hands for dust. The minister indicated where to sign. The photographer honed in to get a close up of the signing. Greta felt faint. She sighed as she rather hazily scrawled her name. She blinked a few times and shivered.

"Greta, are you all right?" Max held on to her arm as she began to sway.

"Uh, I don't really know... I think I need to... urgh!"

Greta swiftly dropped to the floor. As she fell, she knocked her head against the side of the table. She was knocked out cold.

"Quick, get her into the recovery position," Max glanced anxiously around the room. The guests were gasping in concern, as Greta lay motionless on the floor. "It's all right, everyone, Greta will be fine. She's only fainted. It must be from the shock of marrying me!" he tried a faint joke, which caused a rippled snigger around the room. He beckoned for Fab to come over to him. He whispered nervously.

"Get all the guests outside into the gardens. Start the champagne flowing. Greta needs some space. Go on, get them out of here!"

"Okay." Fab patted Max's shoulder. "Leave them all to me!"

"Right everybody; if you would like to make your way into the patio area, champagne and canapés are being served. Max and Greta will join you shortly. Thank you!"

"Oh my poor, darling girl!" Jeanne Standing, Greta's mother, grabbed hold of Max's arm. "What has happened to her, Maxim? I was talking to someone and next minute, Greta is on the floor. Is she all right?"

"Don't worry, Jeanne, she's fainted. She'll be right as rain. Look, can you entertain the guests until Greta has recovered? Can you and Charles do that for me, please?" Max's eyes indicated with urgency for Jeanne to leave the room.

"Oh course, we can! Charles!" She frantically indicated for her husband to come over to her side. "We have an extremely important job to do, come on, all hands to the pump!"

Charles nodded as he promptly tripped over a chair leg and tipped it over, causing the whole line of neatly assembled chairs to cascade in all directions.

Jeanne rolled her eyes and grabbed Charles's arm.

"Come on, out now! Before you cause another mishap!" she clucked at him until they had both, with animated effort, left the room.

Greta was still unconscious.

"Greta? Greta? Can you hear me? You should be careful! " Max leant close to her ear. "You really need to wake up; come on now, it's our wedding day. You don't want to miss it, do you? You've been so looking forward to this day, for ages, haven't you!"

Fab, Max and the minister looked at each other in bewilderment.

"What do we do now?" Fab broke the silence.

"Well, I know for a fact she wouldn't want any fuss," Max held his hand to his face. "So I don't think I'll call an ambulance. She detests hospitals."

"But she hit her head, Max," Fab tried to reason. "Head injuries are serious things. They shouldn't be neglected."

"Hmm, perhaps we should call the paramedics. Just to be on the safe side."

"Max, I'm really sorry but I have to leave. Oh, just to let you know, there is a gift in the hallway for you both. I hope you will be really happy together. Just a shame your marriage has started out a little, shall we say, extraordinary. Good luck! And please wish Greta all the best from me!" The minister shook Max's hand and glanced at Greta as she headed for the door.

"Thank you, minister. We'll be in touch about the certificate, shall we?" Max called after her.

"Yes, I've left my card on the table for you. Give me a ring."

Greta remained unconscious on the floor. Max was handed a rolled up cardigan to support her head. Her eyes, although closed, flashed frantically from side to side.

"I still think we should call for a medic, Max. She could be badly injured. None of us know that." Fab continued to raise his concerns.

"She'll wake up in a moment. She'll be fine... Greta, come on; wake up!" Max gently shook Greta's shoulder.

"Surely you need reassurance she'll be okay? Perhaps a phone call will help?" Fab persisted.

Max thought for a moment.

"Okay, I'll ring for advice. Don't blame me if they want to cart her off to A&E. She will be livid!"

"Better to have an irate wife than one that..." Fab broke off, feeling he had said too much.

"Point taken." Max let go of Greta's hand and reached for his phone.

Max spoke at length on the phone. Fab knelt beside Greta and held her hand.

"Don't worry, little one, you will be fine, just sleep, have sweet dreams, but make sure you aren't gone too long. Max, you know, he needs you back with him. Don't stay away too long. Keep safe… be careful." He kissed Greta's hand.

"The paramedics are coming; they shouldn't be too long," Max replied; his face was ashen.

Fab held Max's shoulder. He indicated towards Greta.

"Stay with her, Max, she'll need you."

Chapter Two

"How was the honeymoon, darling?" Jeanne Standing was desperate to glean every single juicy piece of information from Greta, of the intimate nature, of course. Sitting on a high-backed vestibule chair, she held tightly onto the telephone receiver with intensely manicured hands.

"It was really fabulous, mummy. The Maldives are just perfect; crystal blue skies, white sands; azure seas. It was absolutely fantastic. We even had our own butler; he was so attentive."

"I am so glad to hear that, darling. And how is Maxim? Was he as attentive as your butler?" Jeanne clung on to the fact that she would probably not acquire the exact information she desired.

"Exhausted, mummy. I think he needs a holiday to get over it!" Greta mused.

"Oh, darling! Is there something more you want to tell me?" Jeanne probed. Her eyes lit up in anticipation.

"No, except for most of the time, he was deep sea diving; left me to sunbathe and read endless novels. I suppose I really ought to learn to dive properly and not just snorkel about in the shallow bits."

"That would help, darling. Then you could join Maxim on his epic underwater adventures. Trawling the oceans together to discover new worlds!" Jeanne sounded disappointed.

"I think I'll stick to reading. Max does enough trawling for both of us," Greta replied.

"How are you feeling? When are you planning to go back to work?" Jeanne sipped her cup of tea and crossed her legs.

"I go back next week. Yes, I'm feeling fine thanks, no worse for wear."

"Have you time to pop over to the Island for the week-end? Maybe have lunch out? The father and I would love to see you both."

"That would be great, mummy! We haven't anything planned. We can travel down on Saturday and stay until Sunday evening. If that's okay with you?"

"Of course! Superb darling. I'll reserve a table at the Smuggler's Hide. I'll book you a ferry as well. See you on Saturday! Byeee!"

Greta ended the call and tapped the phone against her arm. She closed her eyes, smiled and visualised her child-hood spent running free in the woodlands and fields around her parent's country house on the Isle of Wight. She recalled the family Christmases that, as she fondly remembered, were the best ever. Christmases were, how-ever, never quite the same when she learnt about Father Christmas, thanks to her younger brother, Leo, and his matter of fact announcement that a jolly old elf, dressed in red, clambering down the tight space of a chimney, was practically impossible, as was delivering presents to chil-dren all over the world on Christmas Eve. Leo's theory was remarkable for a child of only six at the time.

Since leaving the Island to work in London, Greta dreamed about the possibility of one day returning to the

Island and finding a place to live in the countryside. Not necessarily near her parents, but mainly to return to her roots; to be enveloped in freedom and the fresh air once more; to be near the sea. Max wasn't so keen. He had a relatively secure job in the City and commuting wasn't really on his bucket list. The thoughts of dark nights, howling winds and cancelled ferry crossings didn't enlighten him either. Fortunately for Greta, he did empathise with her dream. They had discussed the matter on numerous occasions; usually when Greta was premenstrual or when she was at her peak of passion, lying beneath him in their bed. But, so far, he had managed to sweep her dreams under the carpet, giving logical explanations why it would mean a massive change to both their lives. He didn't want to lose his enviable short commute into the City. A move away would create unnecessary complications on his currently comfortable logistics.

A confirmation phone call later on in the day from Jeanne, affirming she had booked both the ferry and a table at the local pub, gave Greta a warm feeling inside.

"I have invited your brother and his girlfriend as well, darling! It will be a real family occasion!" It amused Greta as she thought of Leo and his girlfriend, Ardi. As a couple it sounded like Laurel and Hardy; ironic as Leo could certainly qualify as a clown, due to his irritating habit of constantly taking the rise out of Greta. Her mother chattered on about the weather and various local topics before Greta ended the call by making an excuse there was somebody at her front door. After successfully ending the call, she sighed and picked up the daily newspaper and began to scan the headlines. She flicked through the pages till she reached the entertainment section; she glanced at an advert that had caught her eye. It mentioned a celebrity spiritual medium that was on a nationwide tour with her live stage show. He eyes scanned the name. She dropped the paper on to the floor and reached for her mobile phone. She dialled her best friend Sophie's mobile number.

"Hi, Sophie; it's me. Listen, I have just seen an ad in the newspaper this morning and I wonder if you might like to come along with me to one of those clairvoyant evenings. It's Nonie Spangler; you know, she is supposed to be really good. She has been on TV a few times. I think it would be great fun. Shall I book tickets?"

Greta and Sophie both held a keen interest in the paranormal. Greta felt she had certain psychic abilities and was susceptible to sensing involuntary supernatural incidents. Max always thought otherwise and brushed off her whims with laughter.

"It sounds like fun, Greta, I would love to; in fact, I can't wait!" Sophie excitedly returned. "When is it? Is it in London?"

"Yes, in the West End; in a fortnight's time. I'll go online and buy the tickets. I can't wait either; should be fun! Speak soon, bye!"

Seizing the moment, Greta grabbed her laptop from the coffee table and typed in the Nonie Spangler website address printed in the paper. She bought two tickets. She nodded with contentment, closed the laptop and resumed reading the paper. She scanned a few more pages to find a worrying report.

'Medium is a Phoney'. Reading the article, she realised the medium concerned was no other than Nonie Spangler. It reported that Nonie had been branded a fake. It was alleged, at her last show; she had been fed information about certain members of the audience via a simple but elaborate sound system whereby they would be asked to

fill in a card about themselves and deceased relatives or friends. This information was then relayed to Nonie on the cleverly disguised device. Greta was very disappointed. She phoned Sophie back with her news.

"So do you think the show will still go ahead?" Sophie was just as disappointed as Greta was.

"I hope so; I've just parted with £50 for the tickets. You can't believe what you read in the papers all of the time, can you?" She sounded doubtful. "And there was nothing on the website to say that the tour had been cancelled."

"No, you're right. We'll still go. Then we can see for ourselves if she is a fake or not; if they try to get us to fill in cards about our relatives, we should give them some duff information!"

Greta tried to laugh it off but inside was full of doubt. She was unfortunately known for her gullibility and didn't want to be impressed by someone who could be a fake. She would be the laughing stock not only with Max who would offer her countless 'I told you so's... but her brother Leo's tormenting would be unbearable, he would have fuel for life. Greta decided she wouldn't tell anyone that she and Sophie were going.

Chapter Three

Greta and Max drove on to the car ferry, which was berthed at Southampton Docks. They were guided by a crewmember to the upper deck. They jumped out of the car, climbed down the steep stairway to the lounge and grabbed a seat with a view over the car deck. In the distance, the Island's rural coastline beckoned their return. The private beach, where Queen Victoria had spent a lot of time, at Osborne, the blue slipper clay landslips around Hamstead were also clearly visible. Greta could see the downs running through the centre of the Island's 'backbone'. She fondly remembered the year she had partaken in the annual charity fundraiser, the Walk the Wight event. She went on her own as Max refused to walk. Greta completed 26 miles across the centre of the Island, taking in steep downland trails, and unlevel bridleways, past the haunted Knighton Gorges, where she twisted her ankle; through historic Arreton and on towards the West Wight along the Tennyson Trail. She recalled the joy of finishing at Alum Bay; her well earned medal she proudly wore and her tired, aching feet and knees, which hurt for days afterwards. She snuggled in her seat with a glowing satisfaction.

"I can't wait to see Mum and Dad again; it seems ages since we saw them last." She looked over at Max.

"It wasn't that long ago, darling; you know, they were at our wedding." Max shook his head.

"I know, but I just love coming back to visit. The Island has such a draw on people. If you leave it, and some Islanders do, it somehow lures you back. I always feel so safe. You always know you are going home when you get on the ferry!" Greta smiled and closed her eyes. She snuggled close to Max. "Oh, and before the queue gets too long, I could really murder a latte and a cake!"

"Yes, mine commandant!" Max mused. "Your wish is my command!"

"Thank you, sweetie!" She kissed his cheek and stared out of the window, trying to get another glimpse of the Island's coastline as the ferry slowly chugged its way through the grey and blue waters of Southampton River, past all the large container and cargo ships, the cruise liners refuelling with both passengers and supplies, and into the Solent.

Max returned after a lengthy absence clutching on to a dark wood veneer tray. He swayed in time with the ferry as it reached the choppy centre of the Solent where the waters meet from The Channel and Southampton River.

"I thought you'd left me!" Greta exclaimed. "I thought you might have run away back to London!"

"The thought had crossed my mind." Max placed the tray onto the circular lipped table. "But, fortunately for you, I couldn't be bothered!"

"You are a tease!" Greta squeezed his leg as he sat heavily down beside her. "Ooh lovely! Danish pastries are my favourite." She eagerly reached out to take the pastry.

"That, my sweet, is mine," Max announced and slapped her hand in jest. "This one is yours." He gestured towards the wrapped banana and toffee flavoured muffin. She giggled at the name on the wrapper.

"Is this for real?" she asked, looking at the muffin that looked incredibly fattening.

"Only the best for you, my dear!" Max took a large bite out of the Danish pastry and smiled back at Greta.

The ferry ploughed its way along the last part of its voyage across the Solent and reached the Island about an hour later. Greta and Max sat patiently in the car as the ferry's ramp was lowered and vehicles alighted at East Cowes. The drive to Greta's parents' house was lengthy, along narrow, winding lanes. By the time they reached the house, Greta was very excited. "Oh look, there it is! Not long now!" She sat forward in her seat.

"You're just like a kid, aren't you?" Max laughed at his wife.

"The Island makes me feel childlike again; I told you that before, haven't I?"

"On many occasions." Max drew up outside the family home.

Jeanne Standing was waiting on the doorstep as a welcoming committee and frantically waved a tea towel in the air to commemorate their arrival. Greta shrieked.

"Look! There's mummy!"

"Hang on! Let me park the car, then you can get out!" Max felt like he was speaking to a child.

"Hello Mummy! How are you?" Greta leapt from the car and ran towards her mother. She was acting like she hadn't seen her for years.

"Oh darling, how lovely! Come on in! Hello Maxim! How are you? The kettle has just boiled, tea will be served shortly!" she trumpeted as Max pulled two overnight bags from the boot of the car and slammed the tailgate firmly shut.

"Hello Jeanne, you are looking extremely well. Must be

all this sea air!" Max pecked a welcome kiss on Jeanne's cheek and she blushed.

"Oh thank you Maxim. Come on in; Charles is in the drawing room!"

Greta hushed her voice into a whisper. "She means the lounge; you know mummy has got a thing about having a drawing room. We'll just placate her." She nudged Max forward.

Jeanne brought a laden tray of bone china floral tea-cups, a fat brown teapot and highly decorative matching side plates into the drawing room and placed them on to a large oak coffee table. Charles, white-haired, slightly balding with a small white military-style moustache that turned up at the edges, got up from his armchair and offered his out-stretched hand to Max.

"Good to see you old boy; how are things in the City? Plenty of business?" he asked as he vigorously shook Max's hand.

"Yes, fortunately very busy, thanks Charles. Despite all this gloom and downturn, our company isn't doing too badly. Looks like we will be in line for a decent bonus again at the end of the year."

"That is very good news, Max." Charles indicated for him to sit down. Jeanne promptly placed a floral china side plate with a cream linen napkin on Max's knee and thrust a fat wedge of Victoria sandwich with her china-handled cake knife on to it. Max gulped. He was still full from the Danish pastry he had eaten on the ferry and, no doubt, Jeanne would have prepared a very generous evening meal for them to enjoy later.

"You are very kind, Jeanne. But I am trying to watch my weight!" Max tried to blag.

"Since when?" Greta looked over at Max with a puzzled expression.

"Since the ferry, you know, the Danish…" Max felt guilty as he could feel Jeanne's eyes boring into him.

"Oh that is such a shame; I spent the entire afternoon creating this masterpiece, especially for you!" She looked down at the slice of cake. "Well, perhaps you might like it later, Maxim." She snatched the plate away from him and slammed it on to the tray. Charles leant forward to take the plate. Jeanne glared at him.

"Charles, no dear! This is *your* piece!" She thrust a plate containing a sliver of cake. It was virtually see-through. He looked extremely disappointment. "You *definitely* have to watch your waistline!"

Max closed his eyes. He desperately tried to stifle his laugh as Greta came to his rescue. "Oh mummy! Don't be so mean to the father. Give him Max's piece of cake, for heaven's sake!"

Jeanne flashed a glare at Greta.

"*I* know what is *best* for the father, Greta! Here, take it Charles!" She indicated for him to take the minuscule slice and Charles meekly accepted his offering. Jeanne, clearly relieved she had restored order in the drawing room, patted her skirt and sat down beside Greta.

"Now dear, before Leo and Ardi arrive, tell me *all* about your honeymoon!"

Max groaned and looked at Charles. "Fancy a wander around the garden, Charles? You can show me how the vegetable patch is getting on."

"Good idea, my boy. I'll fetch my boots." Charles jumped up from his chair along with a cascade of Victoria sandwich crumbs. Jeanne looked down at the carpet in horror.

"Oh, Charles! Do *please* be careful, dear!" She indicated to the floor and promptly dropped to her knees to rescue the cake crumbs from the carpet by sweeping the carpet with her cupped hands into a paper napkin. She pecked at the carpet with her fingers like an over-enthusiastic chicken, clearing every morsel of crumb till the floor was clean.

Charles chose to ignore Jeanne's exaggerated anguish and continued on his mission to retrieve his Wellingtons from the boot room.

"Right mummy; honeymoon… Maldives. Where do you want me to start?"

"From the very beginning, dear. You know me; I need to know every single inch of information!" Jeanne shuffled closer to where Greta was sitting until her face was inches away from Greta's; her expression was of total concentration.

Chapter Four

"They raise their own beef cattle, you know." Charles enthusiastically cut into a thick slice of Aberdeen Angus roast beef. He thrust a forkful of beef into his mouth and commenced chewing.

"Oh Charles, teeth on fork, dear!" Jeanne groaned as the metal of Charles's fork rattled irritatingly against his dentures.

"Mummy, don't be so rotten to the father; he's really enjoying his roast beef." Greta looked sympathetically at her father who was totally oblivious to his wife's latest outburst of nagging.

"Damn good job they make of it too! Carbon footprint, local produce and all that sustainability stuff…" Charles continued to eat hungrily; his moustache rose and fell like little white boat oars as he chewed, up and down, in and out. Jeanne rolled her eyes. It was another of Charles's habits that irritated the life out of her, speaking with his mouth full of food.

Jeanne looked around the table at her family and smiled in contentment. The Smuggler's Hide was bustling as usual with a brisk Sunday lunch trade. All the tables were reserved, due to its popularity. A quaint, solitary hostelry that had stood for over four hundred years at the foot of the downs, which shielded it from the prevailing southerly winds, the Smuggler's Hide held an unprecedented history. Originally a blacksmith's forge, it had diversified centuries ago into an inn. It was famed for its association with smuggling in the seventeenth century and was the centre of local folklore.

"Oh this is so wonderful, isn't it? All the family are together again. Isn't it grand, Leo?"

Leo looked up momentarily from his plate.

"Yeah, spose so. But I must say this meal is top notch. Best nosh I've had in a pub for ages. It makes me feel like I could even put up with sitting opposite Greta for a couple of hours!"

Greta chose to ignore Leo.

"We've eaten here a few times lately and never had a duff meal yet, have we Charles? Oh, don't bother to answer; I know you are going to rattle that fork on your teeth again if you do! Either that or choke on a sprout!" Jeanne shook her head. Charles momentarily fixed a grin without speaking. He continued to chew his food like a cow chewing the cud, methodical and thoughtful, with the occasional expelling of wind.

"There are such lovely views of the countryside from 'ere, Mrs Standing," Ardi cooed from the corner of the table. Demure and petite, Ardi delicately picked at her meal like a bird, taking a small mouthful and each time being very careful not to hit her fork on her teeth, for fear of reprisal. She gazed around her as she silently chewed. "We don't have places like this in my country; it is all built up, like a concrete jungle. The Island is very beautiful, so unspoilt. You are very lucky to leeve 'ere."

Greta didn't look at Max; she didn't have to. He knew

exactly what she was thinking. She tried to infiltrate his mind with her thoughts.

"I was lucky enough to be born on the Island," Greta announced to Ardi across the table. "And I so love to visit; in fact, Max and I have been thinking about moving over… urgh!" She stopped talking as Max persuasively stepped on her toe.

"Oh darling! Is that true? Is it true, Maxim?" Jeanne stopped eating and gawped first at Greta and then Max. "Tell me it's true!" she demanded. Her eyes were large and searching. She leaned across the table in anticipation.

"We have been thinking about it, Jeanne, but that's all, just thinking. We have to consider my work; I couldn't possibly leave my job."

"No, that's right, my boy. Especially when you are expecting a bonus later in the year." Charles wiped his mouth on his crimson coloured paper napkin and looked on intently.

"Poor you, Max. Once Greta gets the bit between her teeth…" Leo mused and continued shovelling cabbage into his mouth. "She's like a clapped out old nag!"

"Oh darling, it would be lovely to have you living back on the Island. The father and I would be so happy." Jeanne cooed and raised her wine glass in a premature toast. "To the happy couple and their return to the Island! But what about *your* job, darling?" Jeanne added.

"As I said, we are only just thinking about it, Jeanne. Nothing is set in concrete," Max tried his tactical placation without success.

"Where would you live, dear? Near us? Or perhaps a cottage near the sea?" Jeanne continued. Her face was aglow with excitement. "I could start trawling the estate agents for you. I would so love to help!"

"I don't know, mummy. We need to have a look around; see what is available. But it will probably be in the countryside."

"As long as there aren't any spiders lurking about!" Leo glanced with squinted eyes at his sister. "Or tables!"

"Don't be stupid Leo; I'll be okay with them," Greta took a gulp of wine. "It was an unfortunate accident, nothing more. I'm fine now."

"Yeah, sure! The arachnid just about stole the show." Leo had a knack of bringing up past events; always the memorable ones, always involving his sister.

"I will be fine with the sp…" Greta took another swig of wine.

"Seeing as you can't even say their name; I very much doubt if you will be," Leo returned. "S.P.I.D.E.R!"

"Darling! Please don't be so beastly to your sister." Jeanne looked sternly at Leo who shrugged his shoulders, laughed and continued to eat.

"This is a beautiful place; just look at the views from here," Ardi swung her fork around in the air and pointed across the valley. "Look, open space, views of the sea; the downs, what more could you ask for?" She flicked her flowing blonde ponytail with her other hand.

Leo stopped eating.

"Anyway, why would you want to leave your comfy lifestyle in the smoke? All those nights out at the theatre, restaurants on tap, a decent job… you would be a fool to want to leave all that behind to come back to this pile of…" Leo broke off as his mother looked at him in disapproval; instead he finished his meal.

Greta didn't answer. She wasn't even listening to Leo. She had momentarily slipped into one of her daydreams. She stared out across the valley; across the green meadows and patchworks of fields, enveloped by lush green hedgerows, that were home to a varied selection of cattle and sheep. She looked out towards the coastline, to the sea and could just make out the chimneys at Fawley Power Station on the mainland. Her eyes were suddenly focussed on an old cottage in a closer proximity. She could just make out that farm buildings surrounded it. She frowned and stared.

"Isn't that right, dear?" Jeanne's voice pierced the bubble that Greta had found herself swimming within.

"What, mummy?" She returned from her mesmerised trance to the table.

"Never mind. Now who wants dessert?" she called out.

"I fancy a walk before dessert," Greta said. She folded her paper napkin and placed it on to the table. "Do you fancy a walk, Max? Leo? Arid… sorry, Ardi?"

"Oh that sounds like fun, darling. The father and I will sit here and let our meals go down, oh and keep the table; you know how busy it is, we could lose our place if we came too. Please decide what you want for dessert before you go and we'll order. What do you think? Ready for half an hour's time. Will that be long enough?"

"I think half an hour will be fine." Greta rose from the table and smiled at her parents. "Quite long enough, thank you."

Max, Leo and Ardi grabbed their coats and followed Greta from the Smuggler's Hide down the main road towards a narrow lane that led down towards the cottage.

"Where the hell are we going?" Leo gasped as he caught up with Greta, who was setting a brisk pace. She strode off in front of the little group.

"Down there," she pointed to the cottage. "I caught sight of it when we were in the pub; when Ardi was talking about the views and the valley. Just by chance… I saw it."

"What? That dilapidated hovel over there?" Leo asked as he threw his scarf over his shoulder, just missing Ardi who was clutching hold of his arm. She trotted alongside him, almost breaking into a canter to keep up.

"You don't know what you're talking about, Leo! As per usual!" Greta snapped. "We haven't even got there yet."

"Well, it's the only place in the vicinity, so I must be right. Oh god! Look it's partly boarded up! What a shit hole!" he crudely exclaimed.

"There's a fingerpost. It's a public footpath that leads towards the town." Greta crossed the road without checking for traffic. "It looks like it goes directly past the cottage. So we will be quite within our rights to walk down there."

"Max, mate. Heed the warning, there could be trouble ahead!" Leo joshed. Max sighed but continued to follow Greta who was striding purposefully down the unmade grassy track, towards the cottage. She splashed in and out of the puddles and potholes that laid on the surface.

"It seems pretty grim, sis. Looks like it's been empty for a while. We can't even look through the windows to see the rooms. Anyway, you don't know what might be lurking about inside. It's will more than likely to be haunted. Whoooooooooooo!" He mimicked a ghostly noise and flapped his arms and twiddled his fingers above his head.

"You are such a child, Leo; one day you *will* grow up! Won't *that* be a shame?" Greta hissed as she fiercely pinched one of Leo's cheeks until he cried out.

"I have to admit that it's a great location." Max was quietly surveying the area, the overgrown gardens and the outbuildings. "There's a lot here; by the look of it, just needs some TLC."

They reached the end of the track before it led off through an overgrown narrow pathway. They stood outside the cottage. It was very still and quiet; no birdsong, no wind, no noise. The skies were gun metal grey and heavy with cloud. There was a hint of rain. Greta unlatched the clasp on the rusty front garden gate and slowly made her way up to the front of the cottage. As she did so, a light breeze blew across her face making her hair ruffled. Max, Leo and Ardi followed in silence. Ardi continually looked over her shoulder.

"Max, mate; it looks like you could be suckered in at any moment!" Leo warned as he stepped over trailing lines of brambles that adorned the pathway. "Drawn into the depths of a festering shell! A costly hellhole!"

"I wonder who owns it." Greta gently ran her fingers over the roughly filled Island stone walls. A small piece of masonry fell to the ground. She felt a warmth flow across her hand, like an invisible pulse.

"Perhaps someone at the pub might know its history," suggested Ardie as she continued to cling tightly to Leo's arm.

"It's so beautiful," Greta continued to touch the walls with her fingertips. She walked along the garden, still touching the surface. "There's something about this place; it seems to be... I don't know... it has a good feeling about it."

"You mean it has a feeling of it being a ghostly bottomless money pit!" Leo squawked close in Greta's ear, making her jump.

"Shut up!" Greta snapped and pushed Leo away with such force both he and Ardi, who was still holding Leo's arm, lost their footing amongst lengthy brambles and ended up sprawled in the long, wet grass.

"Only joking! It's true what they say though, isn't it." Leo helped Ardi to her feet and she hurriedly brushed her coat down to remove any grass strands and droplets of water. She roughly rearranged her hair. "The truth always hurts!"

"Come on, let's get back to the pub, by the time we

walk back, the half hour will be up. Do you know what you ordered for pudding?" Max reached out and took Greta's hand.

"I don't think I ordered anything. No doubt mummy will have chosen something appropriate. A bit like your choice of the muffin intended for me on the ferry."

Max laughed and they walked arm in arm back to the pub. Leo and Ardi trailed behind. Ardi looked around her in a birdlike fashion, adjusting her scarf around her neck.

"Greta is so lucky to have a husband like Max. He always tries to please her," Ardi remarked as they walked.

"Isn't she just," Leo snapped. He kicked at a small stone along the lane. It tripped along the tarmac until it ended up on the unkempt grass verge.

"You don't seem very impressed," Ardi replied. She stopped and looked at Leo. "What's wrong, Leo?"

Leo shrugged his shoulders.

"I don't know. It always seems that what Greta wants, Greta gets. It's always been the same, ever since we were kids."

"So," Ardi probed. "It would appear that you are a little... um... jealous of Greta?"

"No!" Leo was on the defensive.

"But you seem as though you are," Ardi continued. "Is that why you always make fun of her?"

Leo sighed.

"All right, yes, okay! So I am jealous of her. She always gets her own way; even with our parents. She has always hogged the limelight. She always falls on her feet. I have to work for everything; I don't get anything offered on a plate. Are you happy now?"

"No, course I'm not 'appy. I am sad, if you are sad." Ardi clung tightly to Leo's arm. They were some distance away from Greta and Max, who had almost reached the Smuggler's Hide.

"One day, you too will have some luck. I will make sure of it!" Ardi soothed.

"Come on, we are here now. Let's enjoy our dessert! Forget about your worries!"

Jeanne hastily greeted them upon their return to the pub. Greta and Max were at the bar ordering coffee.

"Oh darlings! There you are. The father is so desperate to eat his dessert. He has been staring at it for the last ten minutes. Torture for him! Absolutely torturous! Here, sit down. Leo darling, I have ordered sticky toffee pudding, one dessert, two spoons, for you both. Maxim, I decided you were in the mood for biscuits and a selection of Island cheeses! And Greta, lemon meringue pie and clotted Island cream!" Jeanne distributed the appropriate plates to their intended recipients.

"Mummy, we have just come across a really lovely cottage. It's the one over there!" Greta carried a tray of coffee and indicated with her head towards the window as her parents desperately tried to focus on where she meant. She placed the tray on their table and pointed and Jeanne gasped.

"Oh, yes, I see that little place. I can just make it out in the distance. Yes, it looks very quaint, doesn't it?"

"Do you know who owns it?" Greta asked.

Her mother shook her head.

"Sorry darling, no, we haven't got a clue, have we Charles? We don't know much about this area of the Island. Perhaps we should…"

"If you're talking about that place in the valley, I know who owns it," a voice from the neighbouring table announced. Greta turned to see a middle-aged man dressed in a tweed sports jacket, checked shirt and yellow embossed tie, sitting at a table with a bottle blonde-haired younger woman with a small boy and girl. He raised his whisky tumbler at Greta.

"Forgive me, but I couldn't help overhear you talking," he replied.

"Nosy git!" Leo muttered. Greta kicked him under the table. "Ouch! You…" he nursed his ankle.

The man continued.

"'Tis owned by the local vicar. Funny old stick."

"Oh, really?" Greta was intrigued. "Has it been empty for long?"

"Since the last occupant left this world," the man reflectively replied. "Oh sorry, let me introduce myself. I'm Marcus Mowbrie. This is my wife Arabella and these two young monkeys are Honey and Hector, our eight year old twins."

Greta rose to her feet and reached across to shake Marcus Mowbrie's hand. It was rough from evident hard labour.

"Hi, I'm Greta Berkley and this is my husband, Max."

"And I am Jeanne; Greta's mother!" boomed Jeanne, who had also risen to her feet; she took hold of Marcus Mowbrie's calloused hand and shook it enthusiastically.

"Oh!" She swiftly removed her hand and tersely continued, "Charmed, I am sure." She smiled in anticipation at Greta.

"Do you mean the previous occupier died?" Greta surmised.

"Yes, but in strange circumstances. Very unfortunate… you see, well… I don't know if I should say anything but…" Mowbrie hesitated, awaiting the guaranteed response.

"Strange circumstances? What do you mean?" Greta echoed.

"Yes, the tenant was found lying stone cold dead at the cottage, in the garden; no evidence to say how she got there; nothing at all. Local police won't comment on the happenings. It was all very strange, you might say, like the house... strange," Mowbrie frowned as he spoke.

"Surely the vicar must know what happened to her?"

Mowbrie shook his head.

"She'd been living there for some years. It was all very weird. Folk don't like speaking about it. The vicar don't like to speak about it neither. Always changes the subject, if you try to talk to him about it."

"Oh, that's terrible!" Greta returned to her seat.

"Some say the cottage is haunted by someone or something long departed from this world. By all accounts, they also died in mysterious circumstances."

"Oh my days! This sounds like something off the telly!" roared Leo in hysterics. "I wonder... who dunnit?"

Mowbrie raised an eyebrow.

"No laughing matter, young sir. It was very sad, very unpleasant."

"What actually happened to *that* person?" Greta felt uncomfortable. The hairs on the back of her neck prickled and she felt a cold shiver across her back.

"No one knows, except that she too was found outside the cottage, in the garden. With no evidence on how her body got there. But that was centuries ago, so I'm led to believe."

"Sounds like a serial house of death!" chirped Leo as he narrowly missed being slapped by Greta's left hand. "Something out of a horror novel! Told you, didn't I, sis?"

"Again, it's not to be taken in jest, young sir. That's why folk round here don't like talking about it. You need to speak to the vicar. But he's an odd fellow; I think the word people use to describe him is eccentric. Either that or perhaps a little tapped!" Mowbrie indicated by touching his temple. He took a swig from his glass and returned to his meal. His wife looked nonplussed and smiled without feeling.

"Don't listen to him, dear; Marcus only hears the gossip from the locals!" she added, spooning another pile of mashed potato from her plate into the waiting mouth of Hector, who had finished his own meal and was leaning on the edge of the table, demanding more food.

"Thank you for the information," Greta replied. She glanced at Max; he was desperately trying to stifle a giggle.

Greta shook her head. She made a face at Max, which implied he should compose himself.

"I think we might just pay the vicar a visit, to try to find out a little more about the cottage," Greta announced as she finished her lemon meringue pie. "Hmm, that was yummy."

Leo felt the urge to comment further.

"Do you really want to get involved with a house like that, sis? It would freak you out completely. It will do untold damage to your psychotic abilities!"

"Psychic! You stupid prat! And no, it won't, Leo. Don't try to put me off. You know as much as I do about that place. Anyway, I need to know for myself, er, ourselves."

"Did you enjoy your meals?" The landlord, Jonny Lucas, had walked across the dining room to clear the table of plates. He was assisted by Jeanne, who had collected the crockery and had neatly piled it up at the end of the table. "Er, did I hear you say you wanted to contact the vicar?" he asked.

"Oh, yes, that's right. Mr Mowbrie says that the vicar owns the cottage in the valley," Greta replied.

"He does indeed. He lives a couple of miles away, in the next village. I can give you his phone number if you like." Jonny was very obliging. "I know he won't mind you ringing," he added and smirked at Marcus Mowbrie. "Aint that right, Mr M?"

Mowbrie scowled but managed a smirk-filled smile. He turned towards the twins, who were becoming restless in their chairs.

"Come on, I'll take you two outside so you can play on the swings."

Honey and Hector left the table in a scrambled dash and made a beeline for the door, shrieking with excitement. Mowbrie only just reached them before they tore off into the lower beer gardens in search of the swings and climbing frame.

Jonny Lucas beckoned for Greta to follow him to the bar. He whispered close to Greta's ear.

"Vicar don't like Mr Mowbrie, because he's tried for years to buy that cottage; vicar don't like him or trust him; thinks he is out for making a quick profit; that don't go down too well with the Church. He flatly refused to let Mowbrie buy it. Mowbrie owns and farms the land around the cottage."

"Oh, I see, it's making some sense now," Greta surmised. "But all this talk about mysterious deaths, is that true?" she asked Jonny who was busily writing the vicar's name, address and phone number down on a scrap of paper at the bar. He stopped writing and looked up at Greta. "Fraid it is."

Chapter Five

Greta stared at the scrap of paper that Jonny Lucas from the Smuggler's Hide had given her. She tapped her mobile phone in the palm of her hand.

"Should I ring the Rev… Oliphant?" She looked across at Max who was studying the Sunday papers. They were relaxing after Sunday lunch in the *drawing* room of her parents' home. Leo and Ardi had retired to the lounge to watch television.

"Yes, you can try; but don't forget Sunday is probably his busiest day, isn't it?" He didn't look up from scanning the news columns.

"Of course, yes. I didn't think about what day it was. I just want to have a look inside the cottage." Greta sighed.

"Leave it for today, give him a call in the morning," Max replied.

"But we leave for London tonight; we don't even know when we will be back on the Island again, do we?" Greta wailed.

"Okay, ring him if you really want to, but don't be disappointed if he can't make it. He might not be too happy about someone asking about the place, according to all the gossip at the pub." Max shook his head.

"I'll only ring him if *you* want me to; I need to know that you would be interested in taking a look at the cottage as well; not just me."

"Okay," Max smiled. "Yes, Greta, I would be interested in having a look at it. But it all depends on whether he is prepared to sell it; what condition it's in; you know, all the boring bits that get in the way." Max stopped pretending to read and looked up.

Greta smiled and closed her eyes; she could hardly contain her excitement in the knowledge that Max was prepared to have a look at the cottage. She dialled the Reverend Oliphant's number and waited for him to answer.

"Good afternoon, The Vicarage, Reverend Oli speaking," boomed the reply.

"Oh, good afternoon Reverend Oliphant..." Greta began.

"Oli will be fine, my dear. How can I help you?" Rev Oli asked.

"I am sorry to trouble you Reverend, err, Oli, I am phoning about your cottage; at least, I am told it is your cottage..." Greta dithered as she became tongue-tied.

"I take it you mean Greenacres? Yes, that's right, my dear. I do own Greenacres." He cleared his throat noisily and waited for her response.

"Uh, yes. We were out... um... oh god, sorry, oh..." Greta stumbled in her quest for a decent conversation. "I was wondering if you might be interested in selling, er, Greenacres..." Greta continued to tell the Rev about their plans to move to the Island, how she had by chance seen the cottage and how they had walked to it from the pub. When they had mentioned it at the pub, they had been given further information as to who the owner was.

"Ah, yes, Jonny and Loo," Rev Oli replied reflectively,

a smile filled his voice. "A good man and an equally good woman. They don't attend church much though, which is such a pity. Work gets in the way, I suppose. We could do with boosting the congregation a little more."

"So what are your thoughts on selling Greenacres, Reverend Oli?" Greta persisted. She looked across at Max who had placed the newspaper on the coffee table and was sitting staring directly at her.

"Well, I hadn't really thought about selling it; you see, it is a property which I have owned for a very long while. It's been in my family for generations. I rent it out; or rather I did rent it, until my tenant unfortunately passed away."

"I'm sorry, Reverend. I didn't realise," Greta sounded sympathetic as Max stifled a laugh. She looked away from his twisted facial expressions.

"Don't worry, my dear. I am quite sure the Lord is taking very good care of her. Well, I am happy for you take a look inside Greenacres if you really want to see it. It has been boarded up for quite some time, so I don't know how bad it is, but it does need some work carried out, in fact, quite a lot of work. Oh, by the way, could I please ask you something? Are you married?"

Greta looked surprised at this question the Reverend had plucked out of mid air.

"Uh, yes, I am married. I have been married for just over a month. My husband works in London, in the City."

"Wonderful! Forgive me; what I am trying to establish is, if I did decide to sell Greenacres to you… uh, well, that you would be able to afford to buy it and renovate it!"

Greta was a little put out at the Reverend's impertinence and glanced at her phone.

"I don't believe money would be an issue, Reverend. Obviously we would need to have some sort of idea how much the property is worth."

Max frowned. He stopped reading to listen more intently to the conversation.

"Around the £450,000 mark, if that helps you," Rev Oli promptly replied.

"I see, okay. When could we arrange to view the property?" Greta continued.

"How about this afternoon? No time like the present is there, my dear? I do have Evensong at six-thirty. How about meeting you at Greenacres at 3.30pm?"

"That would be perfect, thank you Reverend Oliphant!" Greta was delighted.

"Oli, my dear; just Oli will be fine. Everyone calls me Rev Oli!" he chimed.

"We, my husband and I, will see you there at 3.30pm and I greatly look forward to meeting you."

"And you are?" Rev Oli confirmed.

"Greta Berkley."

Greta ended the call and jumped up from her chair.

"Seems like you have a new pal," Max smiled as Greta walked about the drawing room clutching her phone. "Was he trying to hit on you? Asking if you were married?"

Greta smiled. "No, course not! But for someone who hasn't thought about selling, he seems pretty keyed up on house prices. Perhaps he just needs a nudge in the right direction." Greta continued to walk around. "It's called Greenacres, by the way."

"Hence the question about whether we can afford to buy it or not. Well, it's just after 2.30pm now; so we'd better get ready to drive over. It will take about 30 minutes or so to get there." Max got up from his chair.

"Going somewhere nice, Maxim?" Jeanne appeared in the doorway, her hair was dishevelled. She plumped the back of her head to refresh the perm. She had just woken from a brief nap. "I don't think I can bear to watch the afternoon film Leo and Ardi seem so wrapped up in watching! Some sort of rom-com or chick flick, I can't work out which! Looks like there are zombies in it too!" She looked puzzled.

"Greta has just spoken with the vicar who owns the cottage in the valley. He has agreed to meet us there in about an hour, so we can have a look inside."

"Oh how wonderful Maxim! I will tell the father when he wakes up. He will be delighted!"

"We'll have to see what state the cottage is in. The vicar seems to think it needs quite a lot doing to it. But we can gauge that for ourselves."

"How exciting my dears! I say, fancy this happening after seeing the cottage from the pub. I'm a firm believer in fate; what is to be, will be, and all that," Jeanne announced. "I will have *high tea* waiting for you upon your return!"

"Thank you Jeanne. But don't forget we are leaving for London this evening," Max reminded her.

"Oh of course; I will make sure it is not too much of a banquet… not too high a tea!" she laughed hysterically and disappeared into the kitchen.

"Your mother is a complete basket case, isn't she?" Max looked over to Greta, who was staring into space. "Come to think of it," he concluded, "it must run in the family! Come on; get your coat, my dearest. Time to make tracks for Greenacres. Greta? Did you hear me?"

Greta blinked and focussed on Max.

"Sorry, I was…"

"Daydreaming? Walking around inside the cottage, by any chance?" Max asked. "Here, put your coat on; at least you are back in the land of the living now, I think."

"You know me too well, darling. Sorry. I'm back with you now." Greta turned around as Max placed her coat across her shoulders. She placed her hands on the top of Max's hands and he held her shoulders.

"Well, we shall soon find out what this cottage is really like. But, please, please promise me this; *don't* be disappointed if it's in a terrible state. This is the first property we will have viewed and, no doubt, there will be others if this one turns out to be a dud."

"I know." Greta levered her arms into the sleeves of her coat and pulled the zip up to her chin. "There's something about the place; but I just can't put my finger on it."

□□□

They drove in silence to Greenacres. Rev Oli was stood outside awaiting their arrival. To Greta's surprise, he turned up in *normal* clothes with a dog collar. Lanky, with a marginally stooped frame and grey hair, Rev Oli's clothes looked incredibly creased and there was a faint odour of mothballs hovering around him like a halo.

"What did you expect him to wear? His cassock? You've got a warped mind, my love," said Max as he parked the car in the concrete yard. They got out of the car and walked over to the Reverend.

"Good afternoon Gretel; I am delighted to meet you. This must be uh…" Rev Oli looked at Max.

"Hello Reverend; I am Maxim Berkley, *Greta's* husband." Max held out a hand and it was swiftly taken by Rev Oli's smooth, limp hand and subjected to an equally smooth and limp handshake.

"Good afternoon Maxim, well, let's not delay any further; follow me please!" Rev Oli turned on his black suede laced up shoes and sauntered towards the open back door. "Have to take you through the servants' entrance; can't find the key for the front door!" he added.

As Greta and Max walked in through what appeared to be the kitchen, Greta gasped. She stopped in her tracks.

"Oh Max; it has such a lovely feeling about it," she gushed, looking wildly about her.

"You've only just stepped over the threshold," Max laughed at her.

"Trifle dark in here; power is off, I'm sorry to say." Rev Oli continued to lead the viewing through into the dining room, again in virtual darkness. "Doesn't help with the windows boarded up. But I couldn't take any chances with squatters. They have more rights than most folk these days. Strange thing, that…" he muttered.

"It's fine, Reverend. Max has a torch, so we can see all right." Greta followed closely behind Rev Oli, and looked around her.

Max hung back in the kitchen. He shone the torch to take a closer look at the walls and, to his relief, could not see any dire structural happenings; not in that part of the house, at least. He was intrigued by the very old-fashioned wallpaper.

"There is still some furniture in here; I must arrange to get it cleared, but the price of second hand furniture is very poor at present…" The Rev was talking to himself and indicating with his arms, as Greta waited for Max to join her in the dining room. "Be careful you don't fall over anything!" he warned.

"Has Greenacres got a drawing room?" he joked.

"Through here, Maxim. Drawing room is just through here!" the Reverend answered.

Max and Greta had to stuff their hands in their mouths for fear of an out of control outburst of laughter.

"Mummy would be the Reverend's number one fan,"

Greta whispered to Max, who had turned his back to compose himself. "She would be in her element!"

"And this is the living room; lounge; whatever you would like to call it; the light is a little better in here. Come on in, don't be shy!"

Rev Oli was stood in the doorway of a very cosy lounge with an inglenook fireplace and windowsills fitted with faded seat pads large enough to deposit even the plumpest of bottoms. One of the boards on the window was dislodged. From that vantage point, Max could see that it looked over the immense overgrown gardens. He beckoned for Greta to have a look.

"Oh this is just lovely; it's so quaint." Greta walked into the lounge and closed her eyes. "It has such a friendly feel to the place; nothing sinister."

"Yes, that's right," Rev Oli concluded. "I am glad you like Greenacres. But I still have to show you the upstairs rooms and also the grounds. Come along now; before we lose any more daylight. The sun is becoming weaker in the heavens!"

Reverend Oli ushered Greta and Max upstairs where they found four double bedrooms, a bathroom and attic rooms. Greta was completely bowled over by the amount of space and the views from each of the bedroom windows. Each room lacked any form of suitable décor and ached for a modern-day makeover. Threadbare strips of off-cut carpet lay across most of the floors with linoleum beneath. The rooms, with bare floorboards, were covered in a thick layer of dust and spent masonry. Each bedroom contained an ornate period fireplace in black cast iron. One had evidence of a bird's nest amongst a pile of soot and dust on the hearth. The odd black feather was a giveaway and a faint smell of mustiness and damp permeated the air. Rev Oli noticed Greta staring.

"Crows, my dear. Always seem to be a lot of crows. They like to build their nests in the chimney pots. Confounded nuisances!" He held his fingers together in prayer fashion and bent forward as he spoke. "Needs the chimney sweep to come over and prod them off their perches with his set of rods; usually does the trick!"

"We could do so much with Greenacres; to bring it back to life again," Greta gulped. She felt a lump in her throat. She felt close to tears.

"Are you all right, my dear?" Rev Oli was concerned over Greta's emotional state.

"She's fine, Reverend. A little overcome, I believe. Greta can be very emotional; particularly over something she takes a shine to," Max reassured Rev Oli.

"Oh, I thought you were disappointed with the state of the place and that its condition upset you. Right, in that case, let's go outside and I will show you the stables and the grounds. Follow me, please!" he indicated towards the staircase.

Greta hung back with Max and hissed in his ear.

"Stables and grounds! What do you think?" Her eyes were wide with excitement.

Max paused.

"Well, it does need some serious renovation work and some equally serious money spending on it. From what I have been able to see in this poor light and in the amount of time we've spent here, there's a problem with damp in most of the rooms. That will need to be dealt with by the professionals. Then re-plastered with numerous tweaks and treatments, I am assuming it has woodworm, judging by some of the rotting floorboards. Then there is the redecoration; every room will need to be decorated; new carpets. The kitchen is way out of date, that will need to be replaced. What else?" Max waited for the response.

"So, it is doable then?" Greta held her breath and smiled.

Again Max paused; he smiled at Greta's unbounded innocent enthusiasm.

"Well, yes, I suppose it is; but the money has got to be right, Greta. This will need some serious thoughts; about my job, money… if you want this to work… we will have to sit down and plan everything out. What will you do about your job? Lots to think about."

Greta took this as a green light.

"Oh Max, I do love you! Thank you! Thank you!" she grabbed a hold of his face with both hands and planted a very large kiss on his lips.

"Come on; let's have a look at these outbuildings and grounds. Hurry, don't keep Rev Oli waiting!"

Reverend Oli was stood in the back gardens looking up into the sky over the roof of the cottage. He appeared to be watching the sun setting over the downs.

"How old is Greenacres?" asked Greta as she walked over to where he was stood gazing at the gathering of crows around the chimney pots.

"I believe it to be around 400 years old, my dear, give or take a few years. But it has stood the test of time, survived numerous wars, storms and freezing cold winters and no doubt will continue to do so. Here are the stables, the barn and the fields. There are around ten acres in all. Not had much done to them in the last few years; just sheep grazing to keep the grass down to a manageable level. No active agriculture though."

"Ten acres!" exclaimed Greta. "Crikey; that's a lot of ground."

"Not for your modern day farmer; but for a hobbyist,

which I assume you will be, it is quite suitable and easily manageable." Rev Oli turned to gauge Greta's reaction. He was met with a huge beam.

"It's perfect; everything, it's just perfect; we love it, don't we Max?" She looked over to Max who was walking around in the barn. He scuffed through piles of dusty straw and smiled when he saw a collection of old and equally dusty vintage tractors stored at the back. Max rejoined them.

"I must say the cottage is exactly what we are looking for. Would you consider selling Greenacres, Reverend?"

"Well, having seen your reaction to the property this afternoon, I will have to say yes, I would be interested in selling to you. But if I do sell, it needs to be a swift transaction."

"May we discuss figures?" Max went in for the kill.

"I have had Greenacres valued, not long ago and the estate agent gave me a figure of around £450,000; but I would consider an offer, in these times of austerity et al. Church fabric funds need a bit of a boost, don't you know. Always something in need of repair, be it the woodwork or the masonry. Would that fit in with your plans, Maxim?"

"I'll need to have a chat with my accountant; but yes I think we would like to make an offer. Will you be prepared to wait for a couple of days?" Max replied. He looked over at Greta.

"Oh yes, Maxim. That will be fine. I'm in no hurry; but seeing as you have shown a keen interest in the cottage, I now feel it is time to sell, even if you decide against a purchase."

"In that case, would you be prepared to give us first refusal?" Max needed some sort of reassurance.

Rev Oli thought for a while.

"Yes, I would! In fact, I would be delighted to!" He held out his hand and limply shook first Max's and then Greta's hands.

"Could I therefore ask you about the so-called rumours about Greenacres? Is there any truth to the fact that previous occupiers have met mysterious ends?" Greta asked.

Rev Oli snatched his hand away from Greta as if she had burnt him. He glared at her.

"Utter nonsense. It is just a coincidence, nothing more. The locals love to gossip and will say anything to keep their shallow minds full of idle chitchat. Take no notice of them; and particularly, don't take any notice of Mr Marcus Mowbrie; he is the ringleader of the gossipers. Have you had the misfortune to meet him?"

"He's the local farmer, is that right?" asked Max.

"Yes, strange fellow; married a woman half his age; has twins," he began to whisper, "you know, out of a test tube variety." He resumed a normal volume. "And she needs constant therapy, of the retail kind; always spending money, bleeding him dry. I don't know how he manages to keep his bank balance afloat!"

"We understand he was interested in buying Greenacres? His land butts on to the side of the cottage, doesn't it?" Max quizzed.

"Yes, he was interested but I am most certainly not interested!" Rev Oli became very defensive and rattled. "To be honest, Maxim, I would not wish to sell Greenacres to Mr Mowbrie, purely upon principle, even if he were the last man on earth! I fear he would only be looking to make a quick profit to satisfy the demands of Mrs Mowbrie. Oh by the way, you didn't hear that from me!" he quickly added and tapped his nose. "Mum's the word!"

Max nodded.

"Right, well, thank you Reverend, for showing us around. Here is my business card. I will be in touch in the next few days with an offer. Thank you once again for your time, at such short notice." Max shook Rev Oli's hand and handed him his card.

"Thank you Reverend; you have been most kind," returned Greta. Her face was flushed in delight. "Thank you for showing us around Greenacres."

"I will speak to you again soon; God be with you!" The Rev raised his hand, made the sign of the cross and blessed the couple where they stood.

Greta smiled and, out of habit, responded.

"And also with you!"

Chapter Six

Greta and Sophie rose up from their seats and shuffled their way to the exit of the packed West End theatre. They trod through empty packets of sweets and kicked spent water bottles. They had enjoyed a highly entertaining spiritual evening with celebrity medium, Nonie Spangler.

"Well? What did you think of her?" Sophie asked.

"Good, I suppose; but I can see how she may have been fed information; that's why I purposely didn't fill in one of those cards. It was pointless anyway, as no one really close to me has died. I just wanted to see how good she was." Greta buttoned up her coat and grabbed her handbag.

"Don't you think it was odd how she picked you out of everyone in the audience?" Sophie asked.

"Not really, it didn't mean anything, did it? I certainly don't know who she was talking about. I think I may have been one of her blips! We will probably be reading about it in the newspapers tomorrow. She did try hard though, didn't she?"

"Yes, she seemed adamant though that you were the one she needed to speak to. You know, all that staring business," Sophie continued.

"She had obviously got the wrong person; it must happen to her all the time!" Greta said dismissively. "I thought she did well, particularly with that old lady sat behind us; poor thing, she had so many dead people wanting to speak with her, they must have had to have queued up!" Greta laughed.

"Yes, she got her money's worth."

They linked arms and strode off towards the tube station.

"How are the plans going with the cottage?" Sophie asked as they found a seat on the train.

"Very well. Max has spoken to his accountant. He has come up with some figures. Now it is just a matter of Max speaking to the vicar to put an offer forward."

"Do you think he'll accept it?" Sophie reached for a mint from her handbag. She offered one to Greta.

"Hope so; he has taken into account all the work that will be needed to renovate it," Greta replied stuffing the mint into her mouth.

"No more talk about the mysterious happenings?" Sophie probed.

"No, the vicar quashed any gossip when we met him last Sunday. It seemed very strange, though. He really doesn't seem to like the local farmer, Marcus Mowbrie, at all. He didn't say why. I suppose we'll only find out anything more when Greenacres belongs to us."

"Do you think there could be some truth in what happened?" Sophie's eyes widened with intrigue.

"Possibly; but it is hard to believe anything untoward might have happened there. The cottage feels so friendly and welcoming; it has a really good feel to it. However, it doesn't hurt to be cautious, does it? Mystery or no mystery, it won't stop me having it. I have Max on side, which is the crucial element." Greta smiled and crunched on her mint.

"Well, if you need to carry out any paranormal investigations, Nonie is your man, or should I say, woman," Sophie offered.

"I bet she charges the earth, don't you? Especially having to go overseas!"

"Its only five miles across the Solent isn't it, to the Island?" Sophie asked.

"Yes, but you would be surprised how many holiday-makers think they need a passport! How crazy is that?" Greta thought back to her numerous ferry crossings and overheard conversations amongst tourists.

"It's part of the magic of the Island," Sophie returned. "Oh, by the way, did you tell Max where you were going tonight?"

Greta smirked. "Of course I did. You know me, I can't tell a lie!"

"And he didn't tease you about it?" Sophie put her head on one side.

"No, for once, he didn't bother. It made a lovely change. He is preoccupied with the house and the negotiations with the accountant. Figures, you know, boring stuff!"

They arrived back at Greta and Max's London home; the lights were blazing from nearly every room. Greta shook her head in exasperation.

"Max is so anti-energy saving; he really moans when a light bulb blows and I replace it with one of those energy saving ones; he says they aren't as bright as the old 100 watt bulbs. He keeps a secret stash of them and instantly takes out the energy ones and puts in a 100 watt one; he'll run out of them one day. Who knows what he will do then!"

"I am going to love you and leave you; I have work in the morning. I need to get my head down. It has been a lovely evening, Greta. I really enjoyed it, thanks for asking me to come along. See you soon." Sophie gave Greta's arm a friendly squeeze. They kissed their goodbyes. Greta closed the front door and unbuttoned her coat. Max was sitting in his study poring over paperwork.

"Business or pleasure?" Greta walked into the study and kissed Max's cheek.

"Your bloody cottage, so a bit of both!" Max returned and looked up at her.

"And?" Greta waited. She perched on the edge of the armchair.

"Seems like we have enough funds to make an offer. Reggie Peabold, the accountant, has come back with the figures and fortunately they all tie up; the repayments on the mortgage; you know the sort of thing."

"Yeees! That's wonderful news!" Greta punched the air with her fist. "So, what's the next step?"

"I will put forward an offer to the vicar. Reggie has calculated we should offer £400,000, subject to a structural survey report. No doubt that will include reports on damp and woodworm being required too."

"And when are we going to make the offer?" Greta sat on the edge of an armchair.

"Tomorrow, when I get to work. I'll go through the figures with the vicar and see what he says. So it'll be up to him, once we have made our offer, whether he is prepared to accept it."

"What if he says no?" Greta's mind filled with doubt.

"If he does, then we can go to a maximum of £425,000. That's it. Not a penny more. My calculations indicate Greenacres is going to need at least £60-£70,000 spent on it."

"As much as that!" Greta was shocked. "I didn't think it was that bad."

"Well, I am being liberal with the figures, better to overestimate than underestimate, so we don't run out of cash.

Don't forget we have only viewed it the once and that was in partial light. It may look even worse once the windows have had the boards removed. We will have to see what the surveyor's report concludes. It will be do or die if the survey report reveals that Greenacres is falling down."

"I'm going to think oodles of positive thoughts!" Greta replied. "Do you want a coffee?"

Max shook his head.

"No, I need something stronger; like a scotch on plenty of rocks."

"Coming up." Greta got up off the armchair and walked through to the kitchen.

"How was your evening with the spiritual encounter?" Max called after her and leaned back on his chair.

"She was actually quite good," Greta called from the kitchen. "A bit odd, like most of those sort of people, but she did well." Greta reached for a crystal glass whisky tumbler and noisily slid three ice cubes into it.

"Did you think she's a fake?" Max turned around to face Greta.

"If she is, then she's a brilliant actress. But there were some things and incidents she mentioned that she just wouldn't have known about."

"Like what?" Max queried.

"She mentioned someone in the audience was standing on the threshold of the good life; a new home in the country."

Max laughed.

"That probably related to half the people in the audience! She must be a dream reader!"

Greta paused.

"That have the letters G, R and E in their first name and that the property has the same first three letters in its name?"

Max nodded his head in approval.

"Well, that would be impressive!"

"Then be prepared to be impressed." Greta walked back into the room and placed the tumbler in Max's hand. "Cheers!"

□□□

The following morning, Greta's mobile phone was ringing. It was Max.

"Hi love!"

"Hi, I've just spoken to the vicar," Max replied.

"What did he say?" Greta held her breath.

"Well, he gave me a bit of a sermon on house purchasing but he has accepted our offer!" Max announced.

"Oh fantastic news! Brilliant! He accepted £400,000?" Greta was shivering with excitement.

"No, he accepted £380,000!" Max proudly declared.

"£380... how come?" Greta was astounded.

"Because, my sweet, that is why I do the job I do; I negotiate deals, as well you know. Let's just say it was down to a little bargaining and friendly persuasion but lucky for us, the vicar is on board! He is very keen to plough some of the proceeds of the house sale into the church restoration funds."

"You are so clever! I love you so much! Thank you! Thank you!" Greta's eyes filled with tears of joy.

"Therefore, it means we now have enough money to spend on the renovation work," Max concluded. "We, Mrs Berkley, are now on our way to owning a cottage in the country!"

Greta hugged her sides in delight and wiped away a stream of tears from her eyes.

Chapter Seven

Max spent the following weeks ensuring all the property negotiations between him and the Rev Oli ran smoothly. The structural survey report, which had been conducted a couple of weeks earlier, indicated Greenacres had suffered historic structural movement but concluded there were no ongoing problems with subsidence. It was recommended that a damp and woodworm survey also be carried out but it was sufficient enough to satisfy Reggie Peabold with the finances and the mortgage company, so he gave Max the green light to instruct his solicitor. Rev Oli was keen to proceed as quickly as possible, which made Max think the sale wouldn't take long to progress through to exchange of contracts. Thankfully there was no onward chain involved. Much to Max's relief, they would have enough funds to retain their house in London, whilst purchasing Greenacres. This gave him plenty of leeway if his employment arrangements should change in the future.

Greta had begun to plan her preferences for the new kitchen and bathroom that would adorn Greenacres. She spent hours poring over countless glossy home improvement magazines and tirelessly trawled the Internet. She had even taken out a subscription to *Country Living* with its ideas and tips on the perfect home and life in the country.

She and Max had arranged for another visit to the cottage the following weekend. Reverend Oli would meet them there with the keys. Max asked if he could bring along his architect to take photos and measurements. This was met with great enthusiasm.

A phone call to Jeanne was made by Greta to arrange another overnight stay on the Island.

"This is so exciting, darling; the father and I are so happy for you both!" The ferry trip seemed to take even longer than before as Greta was desperate to be at Greenacres again. She felt very impatient as she watched another ferry full of holidaymakers idly talking in excited, raised voices about the seaside and their plans for their week away.

"I don't care about *their* holidays; I just want to get back home again," she thought. She glanced over to Max who was staring at her, shaking his head.

"Won't be long now, Greta. Stay calm; if you can." He stroked the top of her head like a dog.

"I like the fact that you always know what I'm thinking." She took hold of his hand and squeezed it. She played with his wedding ring. "I am so glad we are married," she whispered.

"Don't! You'll start crying again in a minute. I can't be doing with that in front of all these people," Max drew Greta closer to him. "But you can give me a kiss, if you want to!"

Greta reciprocated; she planted a long and meaningful kiss on Max's lips and they hugged each other hard.

After what seemed like a very long, drawn out hour had passed, Greta and Max reached the Island and were heading to Greenacres. Greta kept looking at the speedometer of the car; urging Max in her mind to drive quicker. She decided against telling him to put his foot down. She didn't want to annoy him. Anything to do with his driving skills was a pet hate to Max. Reverend Oli was stood waiting for them outside Greenacres; he was staring into space.

"Look, Rev Oli's staring up at the sky again; what do you think he's doing?" Greta was puzzled.

"Probably looking for divine inspiration!" Max drolly remarked. "Or perhaps there are some loose roof slates he hoped we haven't noticed! I don't know, love, you will have to make the point of asking him!"

They joined the Reverend and he held out his hand to greet them.

"So glad to see you once more, Maxim and Gretel. You must be getting very excited!"

Max took hold of the Reverend's hand and squeezed it jocularly.

"Yes, particularly *Greta*; she can't wait to get started the renovations, can you dearest?" Max emphasised the 'a'.

Greta smiled inwardly and indicated with a sweep of her hand, for the Reverend to walk forward.

"After you, Reverend Oli. Lead on!"

Reverend Oli unlocked the back door and ushered Max and Greta inside.

"I expect you would like time on your own to have a good look around. I will be waiting outside if you need me."

"Thank you very much, Reverend. We won't be long. If we *are* gone for ages, just come in and drag us out!" Greta walked into the kitchen. "We are expecting the architect to turn up soon; so if you see someone looking lost, that's who it will be!" she added.

The Reverend smiled and waved. He looked over towards the concrete yard and saw a car drawing up and a familiar figure getting out of it. His smile evaporated instantly. He looked very uneasy. The man walked over to him.

"Thought I might find you here, vicar," Marcus Mow-brie brusquely remarked. "I hear that you're selling the place. After all these years of me asking, tell me it isn't true?" he quizzed, adjusting his waistband.

"It's none of your business, Mr Mowbrie," Rev Oli looked ashen-faced and uncomfortable. He stepped away from Mowbrie's invasive glare.

"Damn right it *is* my business, vicar!" Marcus retorted. "All these years I have offered to buy Greenacres and you've continually said no, you would be keeping hold of it. Then, all of a sudden, some young couple appear from out of the blue and you're selling it to them. You know that wasn't part of the plan. Surely you wouldn't be stupid enough to go back on our… arrangement?"

Reverend Oli stared directly at Marcus.

"With the greatest respect, I don't know what you're implying. The cottage will be very suitable for the young people. They have a lot of plans for Greenacres and they are greatly looking forward to living here. And as far as I am concerned, there is and has never been an… arrangement!"

"I own the fields around here, as well you know, and I could make Greenacres a great place to live too!" He stared intently back at the Reverend.

"The difference is, Mr Mowbrie, again most respect-fully, is that the couple will be living here, not using it as a get rich quick venture, which, forgive me if I am wrong, is your sole intention?"

"Now, that would be none of *your* business, vicar. Once sold, it would be up to me what I did with it. Keep it or sell it!"

"I therefore rest my case," Reverend Oli smiled ner-vously but remained outwardly calm. He stepped away from Mowbrie and walked towards the back door.

"I will top their offer, vicar. Name your price!" Mowbrie called after him.

Reverend Oli didn't reply but disappeared into the cottage. He leant against the kitchen wall, drew out a paper tissue and wiped his sweat-beaded brow.

"A gentleman never goes back on his word, vicar! Remember that!" Mowbrie strode furiously towards his car, slammed the door and spun the wheels across the concrete yard, out of sight. Rev Oil closed his eyes and sighed. His heart was pounding against his chest. He opened his eyes and took a few deep breaths. "But I didn't ever give you my word... or anything else," he whispered.

Max and Greta heard the commotion. They found Rev Oli by the back door.

"Is everything okay, Reverend?" Greta was concerned. "We heard voices and then a car screeching off."

"Yes, all is well, thank you, Gretel. Nothing to concern yourself about."

Reverend Oli stood away from the wall and placed the sodden tissue back into his pocket.

"Ah, here comes your architect fellow, I believe. Perhaps you would like to introduce me?" He smiled cheerily.

"Of course!" Max stepped out of the back door and met the architect, shook his hand and pointed in the direction of the back door.

"Mike, how are you?" Max smiled.

"Very well, thanks Max. Hey, this place is certainly a find and a stunning location too," Mike reciprocated.

"This is Rev Oliphant, the owner. And this is Greta, my wife," Max indicated towards them.

"Pleased to meet you Reverend, and you too Greta." Mike awkwardly removed his hand from the Reverend's limp grip and wiped it on his jacket pocket.

"May I have a walk around inside?" Mike asked. "I

need to get some measurements and gauge the current layout and hear Max's intentions for its renovations."

"Of course, please do go on in." Rev Oli smiled and bowed forward. "I will wait outside," he added.

Greta followed Max and Mike and listened to their discussions. They moved from room to room with Mike taking photographs, notes and measurements by pointing a laser instrument at each wall, as Max described their intentions and the talk became technical. Greta slipped into her daydream bubble, trailing behind them in a trance. Through the darkened passageways from the still boarded up windows, from room to room, she drank up the atmosphere Greenacres was offering her. She stopped in the drawing room and stared into the fireplace. She visualised how it would look in daylight. With a roaring fire, logs piled up on the hearth. Perhaps even a dog lying in front of the dancing flames on a rug, fast asleep, with the winds howling on a cold winter's night. She paused by the window and noticed an old gilt-framed mirror hung on the wall. It was ornately carved, however the glass was covered by a thick layer of dust. She dipped into her coat pocket and took out a paper tissue. She lightly dragged the tissue across the surface of the glass leaving a clean, clear line across its diameter. She looked at her reflection and smiled. She momentarily closed her eyes and opened them once more. Her intention was to gaze back into the mirror. As she focused back on her reflection she gasped in horror. The mirror revealed that she was not alone. Greta's eyes were wide with fear as she could quite clearly see a severed hand suspended by her left shoulder. Entrails and tendons hung from flabby strands of skin. It dripped with blood and gore from the hand. Spots of blood begin to seep into the fabric of her coat and on to her shoulder. It was stationary; then its fingers began to move upward with the palm fully extended. Greta touched the top of her shoulder in what appeared to be slow motion. She turned around and screamed at the top of her voice; her heart was racing and her breath was suspended.

Max heard her scream and rushed downstairs. He was quickly at her side.

"What's wrong? Are you all right?" He held Greta's shoulders as she tried to regain some sort of composure.

"I… I don't know; it was horrible Max, just horrible! I have never seen such a thing!" she whispered.

"Do you want to sit down? Are you feeling faint?"

"No, no; I'll be fine." Greta's heart was thumping in her chest.

"What did you see?" Max persisted.

Greta thought for a moment. Not wanting to dissuade Max or make him think she was imagining things, she blurted out, "It was a s…" She felt the air expel from her body.

"Don't say it; it was a spider, wasn't it?" Max surmised.

Greta nodded. She closed her eyes and bit her lip.

"Thank heavens for that; you really scared the shit out of me, screaming like that! I thought it was something really awful!" He sounded relieved.

"It was!" Greta protested. "It was gross! Inhuman! Horrific! Can you see anything on my shoulder? I felt something on it; I'm sure of it!"

"Most spiders are pretty gross, love. But this is the countryside, an old cottage and no doubt, Greenacres will have a few more of the little critters hidden within its walls." Max checked Greta's shoulder. "No, there's nothing on your coat or your shoulder."

"But…" Greta felt faint. "I think I'll go outside and get some fresh air. I will check on the Reverend, whilst I'm out there."

"Okay. You'll be fine. I will only be upstairs with Mike. We shouldn't be too much longer." Max kissed the top of Greta's head. "Take it easy." He squeezed her hand. Greta flinched as he touched her. She couldn't get the vision of the severed hand from her mind. She took a few deep breaths and stumbled to the back door. She held on to the doorframe and closed her eyes. Her mind was still racing. "What if there is something much more to this place than we realise?" she thought and stepped out into the garden.

Rev Oli was sat on a dilapidated wooden bench. He was thumbing through the pages of a pocket-sized bible. As Greta approached him, he marked the page from where he was reading with a bookmark in the shape of a cross. He hurriedly snapped it shut. He smiled up at her.

"So much to learn; one can never glean enough," he concluded. He indicated for Greta to sit beside him. He looked concerned. "Everything all right, my dear?"

Greta faked a smile.

"Yes, yes of course. I've just had a bit of a shock," she replied and looked at the long, grassy lawn.

"Yes, there is a lot of work to be done; it will be a challenge for you and Maxim. But I know you will achieve your goal. You are both young and very ambitious!"

Greta sighed.

"Yes, there is a lot to do. Um, Reverend, can I ask you something?" She turned to look him squarely in the face.

"Ask away, Gretel," Rev Oil assumed the clutched hand position, awaiting the question.

"Is Greenacres... haunted?"

Rev Oli smiled dispassionately. He shook his head.

"No! Not that I am aware."

Greta was taken aback by the abruptness in his reply.

"Okay, it's just that..."

"Ah! Maxim and the architect are here!" Rev Oli interrupted and launched himself upwards from the wooden bench. He galloped towards the back door where Max and Mike were stood, leaving Greta open-mouthed. She got up from the bench and walked across the garden to join them. Max locked the back door. He tried the handle several times to confirm the door was in fact locked.

"How are you feeling now, darling?" Max put a protective arm around Greta's shoulders.

"Yes, fine, I suppose," she replied unconvincingly.

"I'll get the plans drawn up for you, Max, and email them through. I'll put the hard copy in the post." Mike shook first Max's and then Greta's hands. He declined the Rev Oli's outstretched palm by waving a salute at him instead. "Good to have met you, Reverend!" he offered.

"Thank you, Reverend, for your time this afternoon." Max turned towards Rev Oli, handed him the door key and risked a handshake. "We'll keep in touch with you on the progress of the sale."

Rev Oli closed his eyes and slowly nodded.

"Very good, Maxim. Gretel; I wish you well. Goodbye!"

They watched as the Reverend clambered into his car and drove up the grassy track.

Max turned to Greta and placed his hands on her shoulders.

"Now, are you going to tell me what you really saw in there? I know you, funnily enough, and you looked way too freaked out for it to be a spider."

Greta feigned a smile.

"It was nothing; nothing more than a hideous… you know what. It probably looked worse because it was dark in there. You know what my imagination is like," Greta mumbled.

Max wasn't convinced.

"I will get the truth out of you; even if I have to extract

it from your lips forcibly!" Max drew Greta close to him and gently kissed her lips.

Greta stood firm.

"Seriously, it was nothing to worry about. Come on, let's go. Tell me what Mike said on the way back."

Chapter Eight

Greta's mobile phone was ringing. It was Max. Nearly three months had passed since the property negotiations and sale had commenced. He had some important but exciting news.

"Hi, are you sitting down, Mrs Berkley?" Max asked.

"Yes, I'm ready, fire away." Greta sat down and placed her cup on to the coffee table.

"We are now the proud owners of Greenacres Farm! Contracts have just been exchanged with completion early next week!" Max announced with the faint air of excitement in his voice.

"Oh Max, that's fantastic news! I am so very happy! Ooh! I could cry!" Greta whooped. "I must tell mummy straight away; you know she'll want to throw a party in celebration, don't you?"

"Of course. Right, now the next step is we get hold of Mike the architect and arrange for his team of elected builders to start the renovations. I will let you know more info when I know it myself. Better go, there's lots to do!" Max ended the call.

Greta hugged her sides in excitement. Greenacres now belonged to them. She phoned Jeanne to tell her the news and was greeted with a deafening scream and a distant whoop from her father. She then phoned the Reverend Oli to let him know. He too congratulated them on the successful sale. Greta sensed relief in his voice.

"I am very pleased for you and Maxim. I hope you will be very happy at Greenacres. I will miss the old place but I know it will be in very good, capable hands."

At the Reverend's choice of words, Greta's mind flashed back to her encounter with the severed hand; she shuddered but remained outwardly calm.

"Of course it will, Reverend. Anyway, when we have finished the renovations, you must come and visit us, to see what we have done," Greta kindly suggested.

"I would be delighted to," he returned. "All the very best to you, Gretel! Goodbye!"

□□□

Greta needed to speak with her mother again.

"What time are you coming over, darling?"

Jeanne was in the kitchen, speaking to Greta on the phone and holding a wooden spoon over a large, beige mixing bowl that oozed with a creamy cake mixture and a strong aroma of vanilla essence.

"Friday evening. We have now got the keys. Reverend Oli sent them through by courier," Greta replied. "We are meeting the architect on site first thing Saturday morning to run through the final plans with him and then the builders will start on Monday. Is it all right for us to stay with you and the father for the week, mummy? Well, me at least. Max will have to go back to London on Tuesday for work."

"Of course it will be! Goodness me, I *am* your mother. The father is very keen to visit Greenacres; to see it for himself."

"I know. All in good time, mummy," Greta smiled as she visualised her bumbling father tripping over spent masonry and building equipment and her mother sighing in exasperation as she would be trying to keep him upright and under control.

"Don't leave it too long, dear, or the father will be unbearable." Jeanne dropped the spoon into the cake mixture handle first. "Oh blast!" she exclaimed and tried to fish it out of the gooey mix.

"No, we won't mummy. See you about 8pm on Friday! Bye!" Greta sighed in relief as she successfully managed to wean herself off the phone to her mother. Ten minutes was impressive, for a change. Their conversations normally dwindled around the hour mark and her hand and wrist would be aching.

Greta sat on the bed where she had been packing clothes for their forthcoming visit to the Island. She couldn't help wondering if Greenacres *was* haunted or whether it had been purely her vivid imagination. She was worried and doubts began to fill her mind. She needed reassurance that everything would be all right. She decided to phone Sophie.

"How are you?" Sophie's familiar voice was a comfort to Greta.

"I don't know; happy, scared, apprehensive…" Greta broke off and sniffed.

"What's wrong, hun? You should be ecstatic; you have just bought your dream cottage! You'll soon be living the dream!"

"Oh Soph; I don't know… it's just me…" Greta blurted out.

"It'll be fine; there's nothing to worry about… is there?" Sophie was slightly concerned over Greta's reaction.

"I haven't told anyone this," Greta began. "But when

we were at Greenacres the other week, with the architect, I was in the drawing room... yes, of all places; when I saw this wall mounted dusty mirror and when I wiped the dust off the glass it... there was... this sounds so stupid now, there was a severed hand in the reflection of it. I freaked out completely! I couldn't tell Max; I just couldn't. After all, it is my dream; he is putting everything into this; our future, my happiness..."

"A *severed* hand?" Sophie sounded incredulous. "That must have been flipping awful! Whose was it?"

"What? I haven't got a clue! Some poor person whose lost their hand; I don't know, Sophie, I didn't exactly want to hold a conversation with it! But when I screamed, I told Max it was a... you know..." Greta paused. Her breathing became laboured.

"Spider?" Sophie finished for her.

"Yes, it was the easiest thing for me to think of. No doubt there are legions of them in the cottage. It was the simplest white lie I could tell; you know I hate lying... to Max, to anyone."

"Don't let it ruin your happiness. It was more than likely your imagination was playing major tricks on you. I know what you're like. You are susceptible to psychic things, aren't you? House buying is really stressful; it was probably nothing more than your mind working on overdrive."

"Yes, I do think I am a bit psychic, but for heaven's sake, a severed hand; even I couldn't think up anything as bizarre as that!" Greta started to giggle, as she thought back to her encounter.

"That's it, treat it like a joke. It was probably something that Leo said to you, when you first visited the cottage. Him and his silly talk of ghosts and serial murders." Sophie was reassured that Greta was finding the funny side to her encounter.

"Oh, I feel so much better having told you about it; it was pure torture pretending it was something else. Come to think of it, meeting up with, you know… them, won't seem so bad now as meeting up with a stray hand."

Sophie sensed the relief in Greta's voice.

"You have got a great time ahead of you; all that planning, renovation works, watching it all transform into your dream cottage; it will be bloody fantastic! I am so envious of you!" Sophie replied.

"Promise you'll come over and see it soon?" Greta had cheered up.

"Wouldn't miss it for the world! And don't worry, I won't mention anything to Max; there's no need for him to know about your hand!"

"You are such a sweetie; thank you so much! Speak to you soon, bye!" Greta ended the call in a more positive frame of mind. She rose from the bed and closed the lid of the suitcase with a resounding thwack.

"Okay, Greenacres! Bring it on; I'm ready for you!"

Chapter Nine

Max and Greta stood in the drawing room at Greenacres. Neither spoke as they took in their surroundings. They smiled at each other. Greta held out her arms indicating she wanted to be hugged. Max obliged. Drawing her close to him, he tenderly kissed the top of her head.

"Happy?" His question was muffled amongst strands of Greta's hair.

"Ecstatic!" was the reply. Greta held Max close to her. "I would've never believed that we would be here, in a country cottage, on the Isle of Wight, in the middle of nowhere, in such a short space of time." Greta glanced up at the mirror and saw the mark her tissue had made to clear the glass. She closed her eyes and snuggled into Max's embrace.

"I know." Max stroked her hair. "It's surprising what a little money, time and effort can achieve, without any complications too. Rev Oli was keen to get the deal done and dusted once it started, then there was certainly no stopping him!"

Greta broke free from Max but still held on to his hand.

"We will be all right, won't we?" She sought reassurance. "You know, financially, physically?"

Max kissed Greta in a lustful and passionate manner. He spoke close to her lips amid kiss, "Umm hmmm!"

In the distance was an enthusiastic *halloo*.

Greta smiled and finished their embrace with a brief peck of Max's nose.

"They're here!"

"Here we go; hold on to your hats!" Max walked towards the doorway where Jeanne and Charles were stood on the threshold, awaiting their invitation to see inside Greenacres. Jeanne was clutching a bunch of flowers and a clanking carrier bag of glasses; Charles clung on to a small glass vase and a bottle of champagne. He raised it like he was toasting the house.

"Oh darlings! What a lovely little place! It oozes character, doesn't it?" Jeanne traipsed over the threshold of the kitchen and fussed her way into the dining room. Charles was close behind. He narrowly missed stepping on Jeanne's heel of her shoe in his eagerness.

"Charles dear! Do watch your step! For heaven's sake!" Jeanne thrust her handbag and the carrier against his chest. "Hold on to my bag; I need to concentrate! It is so great, darling! Show me around!" she boomed.

Charles stood to attention; like a life model, he didn't move an inch. He placed the vase awkwardly into Jeanne's handbag and the champagne on to the floor. He fumbled with the carrier, making the glasses clank. Fortunately for him, he was ignored by Jeanne.

"This is the dining room, mummy. As you can see, loads of work to be done. In fact the whole cottage is in need of complete renovation." Greta looked about her.

"Think of what it will look like when it is finished, dear. It will be fabulous!" Jeanne continued through to the living room, closely followed by Charles.

"Oh! Darlings! It has a *drawing* room! Oh well, this is it, then. Greenacres is perfect!" She tiptoed through the darkened room. "What a darling fireplace! Inglenook I believe?" Looking directly at Max, she tested her knowledge.

"Correct!" Max returned. He followed her into the living room. "Just a little replastering and paint work in here; just cosmetics, nothing major. Change of floor covering, or maybe exposed floorboards, new curtains…"

Jeanne continued on her tour of Greenacres. Charles, in silence, followed her like a puppy, obedient and loyal.

"This will be the perfect place for entertaining, dear." Jeanne perused the four corners of the room. "I can visualise the father sitting in front of a roaring fire, holding a glass of sherry, gazing into the embers! How romantic! Oh, and an antique mirror. How wonderful! But it is rather, um, dusty!"

Greta held out her hand and ushered Jeanne towards the door, away from the mirror in case there was a repeat performance from her unwanted guest.

"Yes, it's exquisite, isn't it? Now, come and have a look upstairs, mummy. Let's leave the boys here for a moment."

The sound of footsteps on the bare floorboards disappeared upstairs amidst hoots of approval from Jeanne.

"You've done very well, my boy. This place will be a jolly good show. Do you think you'll be happy here?" Charles asked.

"Yes, I do, Charles. However, I will have to stay in London for the foreseeable future. But I'll be here at weekends. You know, have to keep the wolf from the door, so to speak. Have to be realistic. Still got the London gaff to pay for too!"

"Of course, my boy. Understand perfectly. The way to go though, as you are still young." Charles nodded his approval. "Greta will always have company; you know Jeanne will, no doubt, be a regular visitor. I know she won't want to keep away!"

"Yes, as long as she gives Greta a *little* breathing space. If you get my meaning." Max sowed the seed to ensure Jeanne didn't become an unwelcome pest.

"I'll make sure that she doesn't visit *that* often." Charles tapped his nose.

"Better join them before Jeanne sends out the search party. Oh, and we need to open that champers!" Max led Charles out of the living room. He offered him a hand over the uneven floorboards to prevent a catastrophe. Max didn't feel the sharp blast of cold air sweep through the room as they left. It scattered the layer of dust on the mirror through the air like a stealth cloud.

Greta and Jeanne stood in the proposed master bedroom. It overlooked the fields and downs and faced the Smuggler's Hide that stood on the hill in the distance.

"What a fantastic view, dear. Imagine waking up to that every morning."

"I know," Greta smiled. "Do you remember when we were in the pub? When I first saw this place. When we came down here with Laurel and Hardy. I just knew it was the place. Even from the outside; I could see through all the repairs and dilapidations and all the work that it needed. It just felt so right, so very much like we were destined to live here."

"Always one to go with your gut instincts, aren't you?" Jeanne warmly held on to Greta's arm. "Sometimes, it's the best way to be. The surest way to make your decisions."

"I am a great believer of fate and that each person's destiny is mapped out for them. They just have to find the right route." Greta nodded to herself.

"Very true, dear. It didn't take you long to find yours,

did it?" Jeanne hugged her daughter's arm in appreciation.

They gazed out at the view across the fields and to the distant down land. There was a lone tractor working on the hillside, in silence, with only birdsong that could be heard including the intermittent call and flap of wings of a cock pheasant.

"When did you say the builders are starting work?" Jeanne broke the silence.

"Monday. Max and the architect will be here too. Poring over the plans, no doubt."

"And who's going to be the project manager?" Jeanne coined the phrase, pretending to sound intelligent and modern.

"Moi, of course!" Greta announced. "Max will be leaving on Monday evening and won't be back until the weekend, so I will be overseeing what they do. How many cups of tea they drink; packets of biscuits they can devour."

"Good job, dear. Need to keep the blighters on their toes. No slacking, eh? Lots of work to be done!"

"You sound like the father!" Greta laughed.

"The poor, dear, father. He means well; just gets under my feet," Jeanne sighed. "Still, I wouldn't want him any other way," she added.

Jeanne began to walk around the bedroom.

"Will you be having an ensuite?"

"Yes, and a dressing room. There is just about enough space to fit them in. You must have a look at the plans. They look fantastic. I just hope it works!" Greta mused.

"And what about your job, darling? When will you be leaving?" Jeanne nonchalantly asked.

"My boss said that I can stay on, as a consultant; I will be able to work from home, with just the occasional trip up to London for meetings. I can't wait!" Greta smiled.

"So you will be a permanent resident on our beautiful Island then?"

"Yep! Hopefully, I will be back home!" Greta replied.

"Is Maxim okay with that?" Jeanne gently probed.

"Well, he hasn't said that he isn't."

"Wonderful, darling!" Jeanne kissed her daughter's cheek. "You are such a lucky girl!"

Max and Charles joined them, clutching glasses and the champagne. Max elected to pop the cork with Charles holding firmly on to two glasses. Perfectly chilled, everyone raised charged glasses. Max proposed a toast.

"Here's to a new life in the country; to Greta, to Jeanne and Charles for their home we will be using as a hotel and also to all the renovations! May they run as smoothly as clockwork!"

Glasses chinked and '*hear, hear*'s echoed around the empty bedroom.

Max smiled at Greta who was wiping away a solitary tear from her cheek. "You made it back home!"

Greta mouthed to Max, "I love you!"

Chapter Ten

Over the following weeks, Greenacres resembled a bomb-site. Every room had been gutted by the builders. Lathe and plaster had been torn down from the ceilings and walls, floorboards lifted and removed. The cottage stood in its naked state with bare walls and floor joists. Greta was amazed at just how much masonry and dust had been created. She gave up trying to clear away oceans of it in her industrial sized vacuum cleaner. The builders, super-vised by Mike the architect, had made a good impression with the renovations. They had, however, stumbled across inevitable barriers that held up the work. The outside end wall needed to be rebuilt. Unfortunately, as the builders chipped away the plastered and pebble-dashed exterior, an accumulation of decades of water had soaked through the walls causing severe water ingress and damp penetration. The walls were not only constructed of brick, but of every conceivable material including mud, small pieces of wood, flint stones and pebbles, even a cork! Max thought at some time in the past, Greenacres must have hosted a memora-ble party! It was hard to imagine the cottage standing up against all the weather elements when only a slight gust of wind could have quite easily brought the wall crashing down. Greta decided Greenacres was deemed to be a lucky cottage, remembering what Rev Oli had said, that it had stood up to wars, hurricanes and whatever other historic incident she could think of.

It was late Friday afternoon and she was waiting for a call from Max to say he was on his way back to the Island for the weekend. Her mobile phone eventually rang.

"Do you know the builders stop work at 3pm on a Friday?" Greta spluttered.

"Oh, hello to you too, darling. How are you?" Max replied with sarcasm.

"Sorry, hello love, I forgot my manners for a moment. I'm suffering from exasperation and impatience, I suppose." Greta raised her hand to her forehead. "It's really annoying as they only have another couple of hours work left to do in the kitchen before it is ready for decorating. Now it won't get done until Monday. Ergh!"

"Try not to worry about it. Everything else is going to schedule, isn't it? And they haven't buggered off to do another job, have they? I had their word they would stick with us and not get bogged down with other jobs. They know that if they did, they wouldn't get paid. You have to keep one step ahead of them, Greta. That is what being a project manager is all about."

"What time are you going to be here?" Greta sulkily changed the subject.

"I'm about fifteen minutes from the ferry terminal, so I will make the 6 o'clock sailing." Max checked his watch.

"Good, then you can take me out for supper." Greta was determined not to endure another of her mother's ample gut-busting dinners.

"I'll bring a takeaway home with me, as I want to have a look at Greenacres first and see what progress has been made so far." Max was also determined. He hadn't seen the cottage for nearly a week and was keen to survey the current state of the renovations and whether they were on track for the proposed finish date.

"Okay, I'll see you here soon then, bye." Greta ended the call.

She walked slowly around the kitchen and gazed at the plastered walls. They were caked in a clay coloured plaster, half wet, half dry but the room was slowly beginning to take shape. Greta and Max had decided to use the old dairy as their new kitchen. The existing kitchen was planned to be a utility-cum-boot room. The new kitchen was so much bigger and able to offer a dining area and access to a planned conservatory, a future phase. They had knocked the walls down from a storeroom, off the dairy, to provide the extra space. Greta folded her arms and stepped carefully over the spent masonry on the floor. She walked over to where the old storeroom used to be. She noticed a slight dip in the floor. She kicked at the raised pile of earth to the side of it and, as she did so, a small hole appeared by her foot. A layer of soil disappeared through it. She continued to tap the ground with the heel of her shoe and the hole became slightly bigger. She knelt down and began to move away the masonry with her hands and the hole continued to grow even larger. She got up and stepped back as dirt and stones had rapidly disappeared into the hole.

She groaned.

"Oh no! I bet this is a well and I am now going to disappear into oblivion! Ahhhh!"

Greta lost her footing and was thrust down into the hole, feet first. She tried to grab the sides of the hole as she fell but couldn't get a handhold. She screamed as gravity drew her down and down until she hit the ground with a resounding bump.

"Oh, shit! Heeeelp!" she shouted out into the darkness. She lay in a crumpled heap on the ground. She swallowed and tasted gritty particles of earth in her mouth. She made a face and spat out a clump of mud. She began to move. She was covered in dust, cobwebs, masonry and wet, claggy earth. The hole smelt musty and the air filled with damp. Greta felt across her arms and legs to make sure she hadn't broken any bones. She flicked dirt from her hair and tried to brush it away with her hands. With relief she was able to stand without too much pain, just grazes and bruises from the fall. She looked up from where she had fallen and could see a small chink of light from the kitchen.

"Just my luck," she winced. "Trust me to fall into a well. Urgh!" she shuddered. Suddenly her fear of spiders raced through her mind; she clutched her sides in horror.

"I bet there is an army of them down here, just waiting for me." She reached for her mobile phone and turned on its light. She peered into the darkness; her imagination was running riot. She looked about her and could see countless cobwebs that had broken her fall. There were extremely large cobwebs. Her mind raced as she thought of tarantulas crawling from the inner confines of the hole. Or perhaps a gargantuan arachnid, larger than a man, with tree-trunk proportioned legs that could crush a human effortlessly with a thrash of its tentacle-like leg. She tried to compose herself. "I watched too many B-movies," she nervously cackled to herself. Her mind recalled the severed hand incident and she shuddered. She held her breath and then held on to her shoulder. She dialled Max's number. She was in luck. She could get a very faint signal; one bar. Max answered immediately.

"I have done something really stupid," she began.

"Really? Now that is a surprise."

"Listen, I am in a hole…" Greta started to explain.

"Yes, its called Greenacres Farm, isn't it?" Max laughed.

"Shut up Max, no seriously, I'm in a hole. I have fallen through a hole in the kitchen floor. I think it's an old well. Luckily there isn't any water in here. I haven't hurt myself, too much, but its bloody dark down here and I think there might be urgh… you know what… around. Can you hurry up and get me out of here… please!" she urged.

"I don't believe it! Trust you to wait until everyone has gone home to do something stupid like falling down a hole!"

"Spare me the lectures. I just want to get out of here. I'm lucky to get a signal on my phone."

"Yes, that's a first! Can't you try to climb out?" Max offered jokingly, he was still highly amused.

"Don't you think I've already tried to do that?" she angrily replied. "Not really, it's a long way back up and I don't know how stable the walls of the hole are. I think I'd rather sit tight until you get here. Then you can find one of the builder's ladders and rescue me, like the hero you are."

"Okay, as long as you haven't hurt yourself. I'm on the ferry now so I will be about another half an hour. It should still be light when I reach you. Just stay put and hold on."

"Well, I can't go anywhere else, can I? If I freak out, I'll ring you."

"Shall I ring your mother?" asked Max.

Greta looked incredulously at her phone.

"Do you really think I could cope with her shouting instructions down the hole at me? And the father would be down here with me like a shot. No, I think I'd prefer to wait. It seems the safest option." As Greta spoke, a steady line of sand and dust cascaded down the walls. Looking around her, she swallowed slowly. "Just hurry up, Max. Please!"

"I'll hang fire on the takeaway then. Till we have got you out of your present predicament!"

Greta tried to make herself comfortable on the ground. She hugged her knees and vigilantly kept watch for the spiders. She began to sing. Her mother always said, if she was in danger or afraid, singing usually helped. She sang a very out of tune rendition of the Beatles *Norwegian Wood*, that always seemed to calm her nerves. "I... once knew a girl, or should I say, she, da, da, da, da... isn't it good, Norwegian Wood..."

Greta rubbed her arm. She winced as it felt bruised and grazed from the fall. Her knee was also beginning to throb as bruising and swelling was setting in. She decided to stand up and attempt to climb out once more. She tried to get her foot on the edge of the hole only to find there was nothing to support it, only a crumbling mass of wet earth. Her foot slipped and she felt the wetness of the earthen wall seeping on to her trouser leg. She sighed and stepped back. She grabbed her phone and shone the light around. There in the corner was another large hole; it looked vaguely like a passageway. She was amazed to see it and stood to attention.

"Should I stay or should I go now... if I stay there will be trouble," she sang to herself. "Oh, god! Why me? Right, Greta! Be brave, go and have a look," she told herself. She clutched her arm, swallowed slowly and took a step forward. She stopped, swallowed again and then took another step. She raised her phone in front of her and held it at arm's length, peering around the shaft of light. She could see there was definitely a passageway before her. It was pitch black and draped with large menacing cobwebs. It was Greta's worst nightmare. She willed herself to take another step forward. The light from her phone gave her a little more confidence and she continued to blurt out a jumbled song. She hit her head against the low roof of the passageway. She dropped the phone. The light momentarily extinguished and she was left in complete darkness.

"Shit! This really isn't funny at all!" she shrieked. She knelt down and tapped the ground to find her phone. Her hands brushed against a furry, stationary object and she screamed. Jumping up, she hit her head again. "It had better not be that creepy hand… urgh! Shit!" she exclaimed. "Come on, girl! Get a grip, and find the bloody phone!"

She knelt down again and reached out into the darkness, narrowly avoiding the fleshy object. The phone was on the ground beside it. Greta heaved a sigh of relief.

"Thank you! Thank you!" she whispered and switched the light back on the phone. It illuminated the decaying carcass of a large rat. "Ergh! Gross! This is a living hell! And it stinks like one too, rancid, horrible thing!"

Greta kicked the rat out of her pathway and continued along the passage, flashing the light from side to side as she gingerly took one step at a time. She was bent double to prevent another direct hit of her head.

"If they could only see me now!" She thought of her mother and father and what distress it would cause them to see Greta looking so dishevelled. The passage seemed to carry on for a long way so she decided to turn back. As she turned, she became entangled in a large cobweb, which made her shrink back in fright to the wall of the passage. As she did so, she felt a flat piece of wood brush against her back. In fact; several pieces of flat wooden panels. She patted the surface of the planks and it made a hollow sound. She turned around and shone the light. It was an old door. In puzzlement, she reached for the latch and lifted it. A cloud of powdery dust fell from around the frame and the door hinges screeched in a piercing tone as it reluctantly opened. Greta's heart was in her mouth. "Please, please don't give up on me," she spoke to the phone and clutched it for all she was worth. Wiping cobwebs from her hair, she drew a deep breath and peered around the door. She blinked in amazement. It was a little room, complete with an old wooden box and a few Hessian sacks on the floor. She shone the light around the walls inside and saw a candleholder tacked loosely to the wall with a spent, drooping white candle hanging from it, shrouded in thick cobwebs. She shone the light around the other side of the room and saw what appeared to be another larger box. "Should I stay or should I go now…?" she nervously muttered. "If I stay… there will be trouble…"

Curiosity was overcoming her fear and she courageously walked into the room. Holding the phone once again at full arm's length, she inched her way slowly towards to the wooden box and kicked it. It didn't move. It felt solid.

"Okay." Greta bent over, still holding on the phone. "Let's see if you have a lid that will open… I want to see what's inside." She held out her other hand and fumbled gingerly around the box for a handle. Lines of dust were circling around the phone light. The smell of damp in the room was pungent.

Her fingers reached a small metal clasp. She clicked it open. The lid rose easily. Greta gasped.

"Sweet Jesus! Oh…!"

Her mobile phone rang out its shrill ring tone. It was Max.

"Greta! I've arrived! I'm in the kitchen. I can't see you, where are you?" He sounded very concerned.

"Oh Max, I'm in what appears to be a tunnel. In a room, in a tunnel, under the cottage."

"A tunnel? Are you all right? Are you sure you haven't hit your head?" he joshed.

"No, yes I did! Look, just fetch a ladder and get yourself down here. You must see this!" Greta was in a trance as she continued to look around. Having Max nearby had renewed her confidence.

"I'm on my way. I've phoned and told your parents; they can't make it over. They're going to some sort of committee meeting. I phoned Leo; he said he could come over later. He and Ardi should be here soon. I phoned them when I was on the ferry. I'll wait until they get here, so if we get stuck, there will be someone to help us. I thought it best to have someone else on site, in case of any further dramas."

"For the love of god; are you insane? Laurel and Hardy! Right… I'm not going anywhere. I am staying right here." Greta was mesmerised. She hardly dared think what antics her brother might have planned for her.

She ended the call and gazed at the box. Inside there was what only could be described as a haul of gold coins, a few trinkets amongst them and an old rolled up piece of cloth. A box of treasure. A treasure chest that actually contained what appeared to be something valuable and not a load of rubbish. Greta blinked a few more times.

"This is unreal," she exclaimed. "This sort of thing only happens to other people, not me."

She reached into the box and gently touched the surface of the coins. She inched her hand downwards and it was soon covered in a thick layer of dusty gold. She gently pulled her hand out and brushed the top of a couple of golden goblets. She shook her head in disbelief.

"This has to be a dream… gold in a box in a passageway, beneath our cottage, so bizarre…"

"Greta? Greta! Are you there?" Max's voice was close by. She called out in return.

"In here, quick, you must see this!"

Max clambered into the room and hugged Greta tightly.

"Are you all right? Have you hurt yourself? Have you any pain?" he asked.

"No, I'm fine, just bruised and a bit battered, but I'll survive. Look, Max. Look over there. What do you think of that?" She pointed to the box. Max took a swift glance and then another longer look. He sank to his knees and shone his torch into the box. It glowed back at him in a yellow hue, illuminating his features against the shadows of the room.

"Is this for real?" he whispered, clearly in shock.

"Well, I assume it is. But I can't quite take it all in," Greta replied, rubbing her arm, then her head, which had started to ache. "This sort of thing doesn't happen to ordinary people like us, does it?"

"No, it bloody well doesn't," Max replied. He picked up a gold coin and peered closely at it. "It looks real enough…"

"Hey guys! We're here! Max? Are you down there?" came the distant distinctive voice of Leo.

"Come on, not a word to your brother. We need to investigate this further before we tell anyone anything. Let's come back tomorrow and have a proper look at it. It's getting late now. By the time we have placated your mother and father it will be even later. This will keep until tomorrow, Greta. Besides, we need to drive back to their house, don't we? And I'm hungry. We might have to suffer your mother's cooking. It's a little late for a takeaway."

Max touched her arm, prompting their exit. Greta nodded.

"Okay, you're right, yes, yes and okay!" she admitted and closed the lid of the box.

"Aren't I always?" grinned Max and he led her to the waiting ladder and escape.

Chapter Eleven

Greta closed her eyes. It was quite late. She had just enjoyed a long, relaxing soak in the bath and a consolable meal with Max and her parents. The thoughts of eating a takeaway had long passed and Jeanne had fussed so much over Greta's minor wounds, she felt as hen-pecked as her father. She sighed and drifted off to sleep.

Max was still downstairs with Leo and Charles, sharing a thought-provoking nightcap. Charles swirled brandy in his crystal cut glass.

"It must have been a terrible shock to disappear headlong through a hole in the kitchen floor. Greta is so lucky not to have broken anything. If that had been me, I wouldn't have been so lucky." He slugged at the remnants of the glass.

"Good job she didn't land on her head; she might have knocked some sense into it!" Leo smirked. Charles chose to ignore his comment.

"Yes, she was fortunate. No harm done. Except we have a gaping hole in the kitchen floor. I think it might be an idea to make a feature of it. Put some lights down it; place a toughened glazed lid over the top. Shame there's no water down there," Max contemplated out loud. His mind was, however, racing. He couldn't stop thinking of the wooden box and its contents. He couldn't wait to return to Greenacres in the morning.

"I think I'll turn in now. Got to be up early to get some more work done at the cottage. Goodnight, Charles."

"Goodnight, old boy. Pleasant dreams." Charles drained his glass and held it up to the light.

"Well, I'd better round up Ardi, make tracks too," Leo announced. "Night Dad, night Max."

"Thanks for your help tonight, Leo. Nice one!" Max returned.

"No problem mate, but I didn't do that much." Leo smiled.

Max climbed the stairs and walked into their bedroom. Greta was asleep. He undressed and got into bed. He turned off the bedside lamp. He turned over towards Greta, gently touched her arm, closed his eyes and instantaneously started to snore. Greta grunted and stirred. She turned over. Suddenly, she was woken by the sound of something moving across the bedside cabinet. She opened her eyes and blinked. She reached out and felt around in the darkness for her watch. It didn't appear to be where she had left it. She sat up and rubbed her eyes. The noise began once more, slowly, dragging across the surface, this time of the dressing table opposite the bed.

Greta was a little more awake as she flicked the duvet off her legs, placed her feet on the floor, got slowly up and flopped towards the dressing table. The moon was shining enough for her to see where she was walking. The dragging noise stopped. Greta shook her head.

"What's going on?" she hissed into the darkness.

"Ehhh? Hmmm?" Max stirred.

"Nothing," Greta whispered.

"What are you…" Max mumbled, "… doing?"

"Nothing!" Greta hissed once more. "Go back to sleep!"

She blinked into the darkness, her eyes finally accustomed to the dark. She gasped in horror. She could just make out the familiar shape in the moonlight. She felt her body ensconce into a cold sweat. She started to pant in fear as the severed hand moved around the perimeter of the bedroom up and down the wall, slowly and with a purpose. Greta held her hand to her mouth to stifle a scream that was brewing deep inside her stomach. She retched and gritted her teeth in panic. The bloody entrails moved across the wall in a swinging fashion. It appeared to be writing something. Greta swallowed slowly. She shook her head.

"This is not happening! I must be dreaming! This is just so weird!" she uttered.

She closed her eyes tightly and opened them again. The hand was still there. Gulping in fright, Greta hissed an address to the hand.

"What do you want? Why are you doing this?"

The hand continued on its sordid journey across the wall.

"I can't believe I am talking to a hand? Why are you here?" Greta persisted. The hand stopped; the fingers turned in the faint moonlight. It moved away from the wall and with an outstretched bloodstained forefinger, it pointed at the wall. Greta walked over towards the wall and peered at the scrawl.

"Be careful? Be careful of what?" she hissed in puzzlement. "Why? Why should I be careful?" Greta asked.

The hand moved towards the wall once more and pointed to another bloody mark.

Greta uttered out loud the next message. "Not safe… what isn't safe?" Greta was very concerned.

The severed hand moved towards the ceiling, aimed its fingers upward and vanished.

Greta fumbled her way back to the bed and turned the bedside light on. Max was snoring by her side. She glanced at the travel clock on the bedside cabinet. It was 2am. She ran her hand through her hair and looked around the room. There was clearly nothing there. She walked over to the wall and touched its surface. To her astonishment, there was nothing written on it.

"I must have been dreaming," she thought. She lay back in bed and turned off the light. "Either that or I'm going mad. Where the heck is my watch?"

She lay awake for some time, terrified that something else would happen, but the room remained silent. After a frenzied, heart-pounding wait, she drifted back to sleep.

□□□

The alarm clock squealed out at 7am. Greta was already awake and dressed. She was keen to return to Greenacres to investigate the hole and the passageway. Max stirred. He was clearly oblivious to any of the strange happenings in the night. He looked comfortable and relaxed. Greta decided to make some tea and bring a cup up to him. She crept downstairs only to find her mother already dressed and bustling around in the kitchen.

"Oh darling! Good morning! How are you feeling? Are you still aching?" she cooed and held her arms out to embrace Greta.

"Yes, a bit. But nothing life threatening." Greta walked towards the kettle. "I was going to make a pot of tea."

"I'll do that, my darling. You must take it easy. I'm your mother and I am here to care for you."

Greta smiled.

"We have lots to do at Greenacres today. So we'll have breakfast and then leave around 9ish."

Jeanne frowned.

"Are you sure you are up to it, dear? You had a nasty shock yesterday, a rotten tumble too. I think you ought to rest up today."

"I certainly did have a scare but I'll be fine. I won't do a lot. Max can do the heavy lifting. I am the project manager, don't forget." She laughed and winced as her side ached from bruising.

"Well, I think the father and I should come with you. After all…"

"No! That won't be necessary, mummy. You know what will happen. The father will hurt himself somehow and we will end up going to A&E with him. He's better off here until all the major works have been finished. Then he can come over when the house is a much safer environment. We won't have to worry about him injuring himself."

"Yes, well, you do have a point." Jeanne plumped up her hair. "He can be a little OTT, shall we say. But that won't stop him finding something to trip over."

"And perhaps this evening, we can have dinner at the pub. What do you say?" Greta offered a consolatory olive branch. "Our treat to thank you for all you've done for us and repayment of a dinner."

"That would be lovely. I'll book a table for seven o'clock." Jeanne was noticeably pleased to be of some help.

Jeanne poured the tea and Greta took a cup upstairs to Max who was still asleep. She gently tugged at the duvet until he opened his eyes.

"Tea, Max. Don't let it get cold," Greta thrust the cup near his face.

"Give me a minute to come round," Max blinked and tried to focus on Greta's face, which was in close proximity to his own.

"After breakfast we can get straight over to Greenacres, can't we?" She was so excited.

Max propped the pillows behind his head so he was sitting in a more upright position.

"Yes, of course we can. But give me a minute to wake up, can't you?"

"Please hurry up!" Greta rose from the bedside and sauntered down stairs. Max called out.

"Do you know? I had the most bizarre dream."

Greta stood on the stairway.

"Did you? Do you remember anything about it?"

"Yes, it was really weird. I dreamt that there was a girl in our room. She wasn't very old, in her late teens, I would say. She was wearing these really old fashioned clothes. She looked dirty; like a vagrant. She kept on saying the same old thing, over and over."

"Really? What did she say?" Greta froze; she reached out and held tightly on to the banister.

"I can't remember much. Something about, I don't know… about being careful. She was really quite insistent. Then, I don't remember anything else, except for you pulling on the duvet. Then I woke up."

Greta's heart was rapidly pulsing. She felt very anxious.

"That's not like you to remember your dreams," she nervously returned.

"No, I don't, do I? But this seemed so realistic; like she was right beside me in this room."

"Better not let mummy hear you say that. You know how she worries about the slightest thing. She will have kittens!"

"And that her son-in-law is possibly crazy? Must be catching in this house!" Max laughed.

"Must be." Greta relived her own experience of the night. She decided not to say anything to Max about her encounter. She continued back down the stairs to the kitchen. Jeanne had begun to fry rashers of streaky bacon and was slicing some wholemeal bread for toast.

"I hope you're hungry, darling. The father is. But don't worry, there's plenty to go around!" She swept her hand across the work surface which was laden with sausages, tomatoes, mushrooms and baked beans.

"Yes, I'm quite hungry." Greta sat down at the table and grabbed the morning paper.

"You'll need to have a good breakfast inside you if you are to be at Greenacres all day. I will pack you a lunch as well, if you like?"

"You don't need to do that, mummy. We can call into the local supermarket and buy something."

"No! I won't have you wasting your money on expensive frippery! You have just bought a house; one that needs a lot of money spending on it and you'll need every penny. It is always said the first year of house purchasing is always the most difficult, financially. I am quite happy to make you some sandwiches. The price you pay for a shop bought one, you could buy at least three loaves!" Jeanne carried on frying the breakfast and cracked egg after egg into a small pan where she deftly scrambled them with a hint of pepper and splash of milk and butter. She called out to Charles.

"Charles! Breakfast is on the table… now!"

Charles obediently appeared in the doorway and smiled at Greta.

"How are you, old girl? Is it still painful?" He sat down at the table and lifted a steaming mug of coffee.

"Not too bad, a little bit achy." Greta was scanning the paper. Her eyes were drawn to an article on page 4. *'The Medium who lost her Star Spangles.'* She shook her head. There was another story reviewing Nonie Spangler's latest psychic show. It wasn't a particularly friendly account. *'Medium Nonie Spangler has lost her sparkle. Audience felt fleeced by her so-called psychic abilities. Many are demanding refunds for their tickets…'*

"Anything interesting in the papers, love?" Charles looked over his reading glasses.

"Only an article about that spiritual medium. Sophie and I went to watch her show a few weeks ago. She has been slated by the press. She wasn't all that bad. She certainly has had a rough time of it lately."

"That's the trouble with dabbling in the spirit world. Difficult to believe some things those people say. Give folk false hope. There are a lot of hoodlums out there!" Charles said as he cleared his throat.

"I've always been a firm believer in the after life," interrupted Jeanne as she placed two large plates laden with fried food in front of Charles and Greta. "There has to be something other than nothing, when someone passes away. At least, that's what I tell myself. When my mother died, it was a great comfort to know she was safe, somewhere on the other side and not in any old place, or come to think of it, nowhere…" She gazed into space, still holding a tea towel.

"How do you know that though, mummy? You've never mentioned anything before." Greta was surprised at her mother's announcement.

"Well, *I* went to one of these medium people, after my mother passed away. And he told me things that only I would know about her. I didn't know him from Adam. Nice sort of chap. He was very comforting."

Greta was amazed that her mother hadn't mentioned this before.

"And what about grandpa?"

"Well, apparently he's with her. They're together.

That's all I wanted to know. It helped me through my grieving process. Knowing that she wasn't alone; that she was safe."

"You have really surprised me, mummy. I didn't think for one moment, you would be a believer of the after life."

"Yes, afraid so, dear. I have always been interested in the paranormal. The father isn't though. Quite adamant. He says he will only believe it when he has proof, don't you dear? When you see it!"

Charles looked up from his plate of food, his mouth full, chewing soundly and beamed.

"Ummm hmmm."

"Oh Charles, please don't attempt to speak with your mouth full! Manners, dear, maketh a man!" Jeanne glared.

"Morning all! Am I too late for a full English?" Max breezed into kitchen, freshly showered and looking relaxed.

"Oh Maxim! Good morning to you! Sit down! Sit down! Breakfast is served!" Jeanne boomed. "Coffee?"

"Yes, please." Max sat down next to Greta.

"Mummy was just talking about her paranormal experiences, with a medium, Max." Greta buttered a piece of warm wholemeal toast.

Max looked at Greta, wondering whether to make a joke or not. Greta flashed a frown at him.

"It was truly fascinating, wasn't it Daddy?"

"Right," Max returned. "Whatever floats your boat; could you please pass the ketchup?"

Charles didn't answer but carried on tucking into his breakfast. Jeanne looked awkwardly at Max.

"Let's just say it was a comfort to me and, it still is," she replied and placed a steaming cup of coffee in front of Max. "Anyway, what are you going to be doing at Greenacres today, Maxim?" She quickly changed the subject.

"Probably spend time deciding what to do about the

hole in the floor. Bloody nuisance, but these things happen, don't they Greta?" Max expertly threw the conversation back at Greta who wrinkled her nose at him in distaste.

"Well, both of you please *be* careful," Jeanne sat down at the table and sipped at her tea. "Make sure you don't end up in more perilous situations."

Greta looked alarmed. She threw a glance at Max. Max spoke for her.

"Don't worry, we'll be fine, Jeanne," he reassured. "Won't we, darling?"

Chapter Twelve

Greta and Max drove slowly down the unmade lane towards Greenacres. They could see the scaffolding surrounding the cottage walls. The sun was shining against the metal struts, giving the effect of glinting lights.

"It's sparkling, just like the treasures beneath!" Greta laughed.

They drew up outside the cottage.

"It is lovely, isn't it? I really love it here. It has a certain draw on me. I feel like I don't ever want to be away from it."

"That's because of the treasure. It is making you feel rich already!" Max turned off the engine and got out of the car.

"Right, let's resume where we left off yesterday. I will make sure that we have enough ropes if the ladder gives out on us. Come on."

Greta stared up at the roof. Max caught her eye.

"Don't you start looking up there! You look like Rev Oli!"

"Sorry, I was just daydreaming. I wasn't looking for anything." Greta lied. However, something had caught her eye on the ridge of the roof. For a split second, she thought she had seen a figure waving at her from beside the chimney pot.

Max unlocked the back door and they went indoors. Greta shook her head. "I must be suffering from sleep deprivation," she thought.

They made their way into the kitchen and walked over to the hole in the floor.

"Do you think the passageway could be undermining the cottage? You know, having this socking great hole and a tunnel beneath."

"No. It is so far down. Way beyond the foundations, it won't cause any problems." Max leaned over the entrance.

"But, from all accounts, looking at this masonry, the kitchen doesn't have any foundations." Greta kicked at a pile of rubble. "Look, see what I mean?"

Her foot disappeared under a layer of earth. There were certainly no foundations beneath. It was just chalk-stone and mud.

"The most important thing we have to think about is what do we do about the gold? And what do we do about the passageway. It will have to be filled in... whoa! What the hell was that?"

As Max spoke, a deafening bang could be heard from deep down beneath the cottage. It was coming from the passageway. Greta felt unnerved.

"I don't know, and I don't think I want to find out." She held on to Max's arm as he peered over the hole.

"Well I'm damn sure I am going to find out," he boldly replied and took hold of the top of the ladder.

"Well, be careful, please," Greta spoke softly.

Max stopped and looked at her.

"You are sounding like that dream I had, with that odd looking girl. She said be careful. Do you remember me mentioning it?"

"So you said. But I was just stating the obvious. There

might be a build up of gases or something down there. So, please be careful!" Greta insisted. "I am going to stay up here, keep an eye on things."

"Chicken!" Max smiled.

"No, I'm being sensible, in case you get stuck. It makes complete sense!" Greta was indignant.

"All I am going to do is to fetch that box of goodies so we can take a closer look at it. Nothing more."

"Okay. But I am still going to stay put here," Greta repeated.

"As you wish." Max began to climb down the ladder. He draped a rope across his shoulder. "See you in a moment."

He disappeared out of view whilst Greta held on to the top of the ladder to steady Max's descent. She shone a torch down after him. He had reached the ground safely.

Max clambered through the passageway to the door. He shone his torch in front of him along the passageway to see how far it went. He was amazed to find that its length ran much further than he had first anticipated. The beam from the torchlight didn't seem to find the end. He called up to Greta.

"Just going to have a quick look along the tunnel. It looks like it runs in a straight line."

"Don't be long!" Greta called back. "You said you were only going to fetch the treasure box!"

"I know, but I am intrigued by this tunnel. It is really quite cool!" Max shouted back.

He began to walk forwards and bent his head. The tunnel roof was not very high and it was impossible to stand upright. Max persisted even though he hit his head on countless occasions on jutting out rocks and stones, which showered him with dust and cobwebs. As he walked, he sensed that he wasn't alone. He periodically stopped and shone the torch around him. He couldn't see anything. Shrugging his shoulders in the confined space, he carried on walking. He thought about his dream.

"Be careful!" warned the girl's voice in his head.

The tunnel continued in front of him, dark, into the unknown and a strong smell of mustiness filled the air. In places, the tunnel floor was getting progressively wetter. Water droplets were seeping through the walls, causing Max to think he was perhaps beneath a field. He decided to carry on. He had to know where the tunnel was leading him.

A noise of tumbling stones and dust made him stop. Not daring to look around him, he called out.

"Greta? Is that you?"

There was no response.

"Stop messing around!" He laughed into the shadows.

The noise stopped.

"Come on, you stupid git. You don't believe in all that mumbo jumbo," he nervously reassured himself.

He carried on walking through the tunnel, totally unaware of what was following behind him. At a few paces behind Max, a translucent male figure, dressed in 17th century garb, was tracking him. He was trying to prevent Max venturing any further forward. His efforts weren't working.

The man spoke in a deep and husky tone.

"What are you doing down here? You should not be here. This place is mine. Not yours, mine! I... want you to get out... now!" His voice was threatening. "Get... out... now. You should not be here!"

Max couldn't hear a word of what the spirit was saying. He shone his torch up and down the tunnel; the shadows, cast by the ray of light, created imaginary dark figures. It was empty. He retreated to collect the gold. He hurriedly made his way back to the room. When he arrived the door was jammed fast. Max was annoyed. He called out to Greta.

"Hey, have you been down here?"

"No, I'm still waiting for you up here!" Greta yelled back. "You've been gone for ages. I was beginning to get worried and I couldn't get a signal on my stupid phone."

"Well this bloody door to the treasure is stuck. I can't open it!" Max shouted in frustration. "And I have just heard this… oh, it doesn't matter. Can you fetch an axe for me? I need to get this door open!"

"Hang on, I'll go and find one and throw it down the hole for you," Greta shouted from the kitchen and dashed off in search of an axe. Greta shook her head; Max was always so specific; she had no idea where to find such a tool. She came across one of the builder's toolboxes, crouched down on the floor and opened the lid. She rattled her way through various spanners, hammers and chisels. Unfortunately there wasn't an axe. She decided that a claw hammer would have to suffice. She closed the toolbox lid and walked back to the hole in the floor.

As he waited for Greta, Max thought about his eerie encounter in the tunnel. He decided not to tell Greta about it. He felt he must have imagined it. There was clearly nothing in the tunnel and there was no way, whatever it was, could have left without getting past Greta, unless there was another way out. He convinced himself it must have been rats. Nothing more. He heard the thud of a tool hitting the ground and walked over to retrieve it. Holding the hammer in annoyance, he looked up towards Greta, who was perched over the entrance.

"I asked for an axe! Are you all right?" he called.

"Couldn't find one, sorry," Greta replied. "Yeah, I'm fine. Just waiting for you to bring the booty up," she smiled. "I am getting really excited about it now!"

"Okay, I'll be back in a moment. Once I get this door open."

"It must have jammed last night, when we left," Greta added. She knew, however, that the door had been left open.

"Hmm, something like that," Max's voice became muffled as he walked away from Greta.

Max began to relentlessly beat the hammer against the latch, which remained tightly closed. Sparks from the metal being hit upon metal cascaded in the semi-darkness as he worked to release the door. After a good ten minutes of labour, he sat down on the ground, out of breath. "This is crazy!" he thought. "It just doesn't want to budge. Something is stopping it." He got up and threw his weight against the door. It still held hard. Max was becoming tired. He leant against the wall of the tunnel and wiped his forehead.

"How are you getting on? Have you opened it yet?" Greta yelled down into the hole.

"No, it's not moving an inch!"

"Shall I come down to see if I can help?" Greta suggested.

"Sure, try your luck. You might have the magic touch!" Max sarcastically replied. "Don't fall down the hole this time! Use the ladder!"

Greta carefully made her descent from the kitchen, looking down at each rung of the ladder before she slowly placed her foot down. She eventually joined Max in the tunnel.

"Yesterday, it was fine; it opened with only minimal effort. I wonder why it won't open now." Greta took hold of the latch and pulled.

"You tell me. It's as if something is trying to stop us getting inside."

Greta opened her mouth to speak but decided against it. She heaved with all her might on the latch. On the second attempt the latch gave way and creaked open.

"Well, you certainly do have the magic touch, well done, love!" Max was relieved but a little perturbed his wife had been the one to open the door.

Greta was reluctant to step inside.

"I wonder if it wouldn't open for a reason. It's like we were prevented from entering; from taking the box of gold. Do you think it's a sign, Max?"

"No, I don't think so. After all, we, well, *you* made the discovery in the first place didn't you? That was meant to happen, to bring us to this tunnel and find the treasure. If you hadn't have fallen through the floor then we would have been none the wiser of what was lying underneath the cottage." Max felt the need to inject some positive vibes to the situation.

"Suppose so," Greta looked to the floor. "Do you mind going inside to get the box, I don't want to. I get this feeling that something isn't right. Stupid of me, but my gut instinct is telling us to get the hell out of here and leave the box where it is."

"You aren't serious, surely?" Max stopped in the doorway. "What's making you feel like that?"

"I don't know, I just have this overwhelming feeling... I feel really spooked."

"Is that because I told you about my dream of that girl?" Max quizzed.

"It might be. But..." Greta swallowed slowly. "Well, I wasn't going to tell you this, but last night... I experienced something... similar." She elaborated on the truth somewhat. "It was a dream, although it felt like it... I mean, well, it, er, the girl, was possibly the same girl as you saw in your dream, was actually in the our room. It read -

sorry - *said*… the same thing to me to *be careful*. I didn't say anything to you this morning as I thought you wouldn't believe me. It must be a coincidence. They say married couples tend to think along the same lines."

"You aren't making an awful lot of sense. Read? What did it read?" Max was confused. "And, yes, we might be on the same wavelength, but after being together considerably longer than we already have." Max was intrigued that Greta had the same experience. "You know I am not one for all that spooky stuff and that I will only believe in ghosts if I see one. I can honestly say that at this present moment, I still remain unconvinced. But what you were saying earlier, about it read…?" Max folded his arms.

"Oh nothing, I was getting muddled up. So what about the noise down here, earlier?" Greta was unnerved.

"Noise? Oh probably rats. Nothing more; nothing to worry about." Max shrugged off Greta's concerns.

"Well, that's definitely made my mind up," Greta shuddered. "I am getting out of here, right now! And you must too. Sod the gold. Rats, spooks, it's all too much for me. To think there might be something down here is completely freakish. And why was the door jammed shut? I don't like this at all, Max. I am baling out, right now!"

"But you opened it…" Max called after Greta who was already bumbling back along the passageway to the ladder, flicking cobwebs from her hair and shuddering as she did so.

"Never been so bloody sure in all my life!" she yelled.

"What about the box of booty that could change your life?" Max looked back down the passageway.

"I am happy enough with my life without it, or any ghosts, thanks very much!"

"But I'm not," muttered Max. "A strange noise or two won't stop me!" He grabbed the edge of the door and pulled it open. To his amazement, the door appeared to come to life and violently slammed in front of him, narrowly missing taking the tips of his fingers off. It made rivers of dust and sand fall from around the frame. Max jumped back in shock. "Well, perhaps that might just stop me for today!" he decided and stumbled back towards the ladder. "I think I need a Scotch!"

Chapter Thirteen

Max and Greta had arrived back at Greta's parents' home and were relaxing in the lounge. They both clutched a tumbler of whisky. Greta was sat at Max's feet.

"So, what did you think of today's excitement? We didn't achieve much, did we?" Max stroked the top of Greta's head. They were gazing into the dying embers of the open fire.

"No. But I am beginning to wonder if Reverend Oli does know something about Greenacres. Perhaps he does know, as we seem to be discovering, that it has a sinister side." Greta didn't blink as she spoke. She continued to stare at the fire.

"Of course he does. He wouldn't have told us anything bad about the place, would he? It would naturally have put us off buying it. He wouldn't have risked losing a sale."

"It's not fair though, is it? We have bought a lovely old cottage. Renovating it to our spec and then we come across all this." Greta had tears in her eyes.

"It's only a small barrier, darling. Life is full of them; we just have to find a way to overcome it. This'll be a walk in the park." Max continued to stroke Greta's hair.

"Barrier? More like the old Berlin Wall! I can't see a way around it, over it, under it..."

"It was only a noise. Let's see what happens this week. The builders are back tomorrow, aren't they? We'll get them to have a look at the possibility of redesigning the hole to make it look like a well. I am going back to London tomorrow lunchtime. I will go over there first thing tomorrow morning, so I can oversee what they are doing. Give you a bit of support."

Greta wasn't listening. She sat bolt upright and exclaimed.

"Of course! It is staring me in the face… Nonie Spangler!"

"Who?" Max looked perplexed.

"Nonie Spangler, the medium. The person whose psychic show Sophie and I went to… the other week!"

"Oh, the fake medium!" Max laughed. "Why on earth are you thinking about her?"

"She might be able to help us," Greta stood up with her back to the fireplace.

"What with? The building work? I think I have a spare safety helmet she can use!" Max took another slug of whisky.

"Don't be so silly. She might be able to put some light on that girl we both think we saw or heard, the other night. And the noise in the tunnel!" Greta paced around the room.

"Whatever you wish, my dearest. But I think you will be just wasting your time and money. She will probably tell you a pack of lies. Like most of those people do. Perhaps I should become a spiritual medium and con people out of pots of money and tell them about their dead relatives."

"Oh Max, grow up, will you?" Greta growled. She couldn't bear to look at his facial expression. If she did look at him, she would have quite happily wiped the smirk off his face with one fell swoop of her hand.

"Get this Nonie person over here then, if it makes you happy. But don't come crying to me if she doesn't come up with anything. The media seem to think she is a total fake. So do her fans now, according to the papers."

"Well, then perhaps we will be the people to prove the press wrong!" Greta snapped.

"I also think we ought to speak to the Reverend Oli. Try to glean some more information from him. He might be able to provide some sort of divine intervention."

"What do you mean?" Greta frowned.

"Get him to perform an exorcism!" Max chuckled.

"So you *do* think there is something down there then?" Greta's eyes widened with intrigue.

"I give up! Whatever I suggest, you just throw it back at me. I thought that it would be cheaper to have him come over and make a donation to the Church, rather than pay the price of a celebrity spook shuffler. Anyway, its late, I'm off to bed. That is, if it's convenient with you?" Max rose from the sofa and carried his glass to the kitchen, rinsed it under the tap and placed it on the draining board with defiant thump.

Greta shook her head. She hated it when Max disagreed with her. She felt belittled that he found it great sport to scoff at her feelings and thoughts. She bent down and poked the fire with ferocity. "Errr!" she growled into the dying embers.

□□□

Max was pretending to be asleep when Greta walked into their bedroom. Her parents had long since retired and the sound of steady, muffled snoring was coming from behind their bedroom door.

"Night, Max. Pleasant dreams!" Greta hissed.

Max didn't reply. He felt it would only spark off another hostile reaction.

□□□

It was around 2am when Greta found herself being woken up by a strange noise. It sounded like something shuffling across the ceiling. She was still half asleep when she heard a voice softly calling her.

"Greta... Greta. Please, please be very, very careful..." The voice was pleading with her.

"Wha... who is that? What are you?" Greta drew the duvet around her head.

"My name is Willow. Please be careful, Greta. I heed a warning to you," Willow's voice softly echoed around the room.

"Where are you from, Willow? How do you know my name?" Greta struggled to sit up right in bed.

"Shushhhh..." Willow hissed. "I am from the other world. But I used to live at Greenacres."

Greta was alarmed.

"Greenacres? When did you live at Greenacres? And why are you here at my parents' house?"

Willow paused.

"I lived there many, many years ago, with my mother and father. But they died and left me there alone. I was only young."

"How did they die?" Greta was intrigued.

"Consumption; they died within hours of each other. I tried to care for them then, they left me... all alone."

"Are you with them now, Willow?" Greta felt compelled to continue the conversation.

"I see them, sometimes, yes."

"How did you die, Willow? Greta asked.

There was no response.

"Willow? Are you still there?"

"Yes," sobbed the reluctant reply. "I... I... was murdered."

Greta was horrified.

"What? Oh, you poor love! Who did it? Do you know?" Greta felt tears stinging in her eyes.

"It was him... the man," Willow sobbed. "He killed me. I was only young. I cannot rest because he is still here! He is scaring me!"

"Do you know this man?" Greta wiped the corner of her eyes. "I will help you! I will try, I promise."

"I must go now. I see him. He is coming for me... I must go. Greta, remember, please, be careful!"

"Willow? Willow? Come back! Come back! I need to find out more from you!" Greta yelled. She felt a hand on her arm and she shrieked.

"It's all right. It's me, Max. You were having a nightmare, love. Come on, give me a cuddle. It's all right."

Max was holding Greta in his arms and he was stroking her hair. Greta was horrified. She was shaking in fright.

"It was her, Max. It was the girl... again." Greta clung tightly to Max.

"Who?"

"Her name is Willow. It is the same person I, we, saw last night. Here in this room. She was right here. She was telling me everything. She told me about her parents, how she died, where she lived... then she went away... said that *he* was after her. Max, I need to help her!" Greta was trembling.

Max held firmly on to Greta's arms.

"You were dreaming, love. This Willow girl was only in your dream. She probably doesn't even exist. It's all to do with what happened yesterday, it's played on your mind so much, you've dreamt about it, probably because I mentioned her as well. You've got yourself into a complete tizzy with this ghost thing. You mustn't let it take over your life."

"But it was so real, Max. She seemed so real. I was communicating with her. I could hear her, as plain as day. She was telling me again to be careful. I need to find her."

"Well, she isn't here in this room, is she? Look," Max turned on the bedside lamp and indicated around the room with a sweep of his hand. It was empty.

"This is so bizarre!" Greta shook her head in despair. "But I want to get to the bottom of all this. I am going to ring Nonie Spangler in the morning and get her to come over to Greenacres. Just for my piece of mind, if nothing else."

"Okay. Try to get some sleep. Its only 2.30 in the morning." Max squeezed Greta's shoulder, reached over and turned off the light. "I'm surprised your mother didn't hear you shout!"

Greta wiped her eyes and laid her head back onto her pillows. She refused to go back to sleep just in case Willow reappeared. She was confused over the fact that Willow had appeared at her parent's home and not at Greenacres. How did she know where Greta was? After an hour of waiting, she gave up, disappointed that Willow did not return.

Chapter Fourteen

"It was as plain as day, Sophie. She was telling me about how she was murdered, and then she just went... disappeared...into the darkness," Greta recounted her experience over her mobile phone the following morning.

"So, now its time to bring in the cavalry," Sophie announced.

"Yes, I phoned Nonie Spangler earlier, spoke at length to her and she has agreed to travel over later this afternoon. I have an appointment with her at 4 o'clock."

"Lucky she could fit you into her busy schedule, with all those shows. Let's hope you will get some answers. I think she'll be okay. She'll hopefully prove her worth and gift of being a medium, if she does uncover something. Remember; don't give her any clues about Willow. Let her work everything out for herself. Then you will know if she is the real thing or not. Is Max going to be there?"

"No, he's going back to London at lunchtime. So it's just going to be me here at Greenacres."

"Will it help if your mum is with you? For moral support?" Sophie proffered.

"What do you think? It will end up being the Jeanne Standing show. I won't be able to get a word in edgeways. No, it isn't a good idea. It such a shame you can't come over."

"I know, work beckons, hun. I would love to come otherwise. I like a bit of the old supernatural stuff, as you know. But please, keep me posted. I'm only at the end of the phone if you need me."

"Thanks, Soph, you are a true friend. I'll let you know all about it. I'll ring you tonight."

Greta walked into the kitchen. She glanced at her watch, it was nearly 3 o'clock. The builders were tidying up, having finished plastering the walls. The gaffer was washing his hands in an old bucket. He looked up to Greta.

"That's us done for the day, Mrs Berkley. I think what we discussed about the well is the best solution. I'll get a quote together and let you know the cost in the next few days. It'll make a lovely feature. Just needs a bit of water in it!" he joked.

"Yes, right, thank you very much. I'll see you tomorrow morning. Bright and early!" Greta walked him to the door. She was anxious to get rid of the builders before Nonie's arrival.

"Bye!" She slammed the door behind them as they congregated outside, lighting cigarettes and adjusting their trouser waistlines to a respectable level, higher up from the previous position of the crease line of their backsides.

A few minutes after 4pm, a small, unassuming car drew up outside Greenacres and an equally small and unassuming woman emerged. She clung tightly to an oversized green handbag and the car keys, with her other hand she adjusted her stringed pearls around her neck. She appeared awkward and nervous. Greta stood at the doorway to greet her.

"Hello, are you Greta?" Nonie Spangler panted. "Sorry, couldn't find you straight away. The *sat nav* wasn't much help. How do you do? I'm Nonie Spangler." She shook Greta's hand with enthusiasm.

"Hello, yes, I'm Greta. Please, come in. May I call you Nonie?" Greta couldn't help but take an instant liking to this rather odd little character.

"Yes, that will be fine, dear. Now, how can I help you?" She beamed up at Greta like an expectant child and blinked several times.

"I'm not sure, but I think we might have an, erm, ghost. I'd like you to see if you can find anything."

"Right. Not much to go on, but I will give it my best shot. Have you lived here long?" Nonie started to wander slowly around the hallway.

"We don't actually live here yet. The cottage is still undergoing the last stages of renovation work. But we hope to move in very soon," Greta replied, intrigued that Nonie was touching the walls with one hand on top of the other. She bit her lip. Thoughts of a Basil Fawlty sketch ran through her mind.

"Oh, I see. May I go into this room?" Nonie pointed to the drawing room.

"Yes, please do." Greta followed at a safe distance; she was intrigued.

There was a break in the conversation. Nonie was standing in the centre of the room looking at the fireplace. She appeared to be in a trance.

"Do you…" Greta began.

"Shush, dear. I think there might be something here." Nonie's eyes were wide as she spoke. She started to breath heavily. She clutched at her pearl necklace.

"Okay, right," Greta wasn't convinced.

"Perhaps not," Nonie walked towards the door. "Something is drawing me to the kitchen. Can I go through?" She walked around as though she knew the layout of the house.

"Be careful, there is still work being done there…" Greta called out.

"Ah, yes of course, *be careful*," Nonie carried on walking, gazing at the ceilings of each room.

Nonie made a gasping sound as she walked into the kitchen. Greta was alarmed.

"Have you seen something?"

"Nothing yet, my dear. My asthma plays up from time to time." Nonie drew a sharp intake of breath on an inhaler. "Must be all this dust!"

Greta shook her head. Perhaps Max was right and that Nonie was a complete waste of time and money.

"Oh, I say, that's a big hole in the floor, dear," Nonie exclaimed as she hastily replaced her inhaler into her handbag.

"Yes, we're going to make a feature of it," Greta sighed. She was becoming bored. She leant against the worktop and folded her arms.

"Good idea, but don't do anything about it until you are absolutely sure," Nonie turned and looked at her. She fiddled nervously with her pearls.

Greta's heart beat faster.

"What do you mean?" She was intrigued.

"Before you cover it over," Nonie replied.

"I didn't say we would be…" Greta was puzzled.

"Not an idea, don't cover it over, until you are absolutely *sure*, dear," Nonie reiterated.

"Right, so have you found something?"

"Not exactly dear, but something has possibly found *you*." Nonie stared into the hole. "I am being told for some reason, to tell you, to be careful. There is nothing more."

"Who told you that?" Greta felt Nonie had discovered Willow.

"Not sure, my dear. I can hear voices. There is more

than one voice. A girl's voice or perhaps a woman's voice; but they seem to be talking over one another."

"So you can't put names to any of the voices?" Greta felt cheated.

"No, my dear. I'm sorry. They won't tell me anything." Nonie began to search through her handbag and recovered her car key. "There's no point hanging around for nothing, is there?"

"Oh, is that it? You haven't been here for long." Greta was surprised at the briefness of the visit. "Well, you've been of some help, I think. I appreciate you coming over. I thought you might have stayed a little bit longer." Greta escorted Nonie to the back door.

"Pleasure to have met you, Greta. My fee is £50, by the way; I prefer cash. And, if you need any further assistance, ring me. I'll be only too happy to return." Nonie smiled as she held out her hand to collect her fee.

Greta gulped and tried not to look too shocked.

"£50? But… is that it? Oh, oh okay." She pulled out her purse and flicked off two twenty pound and one ten pound note from a roll of notes. She felt reluctant to hand the money over. In fact, she felt cheated. She didn't say anything as Nonie virtually snatched the notes from Greta's hand. She decided not to offer any information on costs to Max unless he asked her. Her gullibility was shining through once more and she shook her head in annoyance at her inability to question Nonie's extortionate fee.

"Goodbye." Greta closed the door and sighed in disappointment. She watched Nonie tiptoe through the lengthening grass on the back lawn to her car. She turned and waved. Greta didn't feel Nonie had contributed anything more than she already knew. In fact, Greta was one step in front of her, as Willow didn't offer her name. Greta didn't see Nonie staring at the roof of the cottage before she got into her car. She also didn't notice that Nonie's car had stopped half way up the lane where Marcus Mowbrie was stood, blocking her way.

"Good afternoon! Sorry to bother you... uh, but have you just been to see Mrs Berkley?" Mowbrie began the conversation.

"Yes," Nonie replied, annoyed at his approach.

"I'm the local farmer; I own the fields around here, around Greenacres. You see, I recognise you from somewhere, you're a medium aren't you?" he continued. "I've seen you on the telly. I thought you were rather good," he enthused.

Nonie smiled in appreciation without speaking.

"Mrs Berkley has a problem, does she?" he probed.

"It's not for me to say, uh, Mr... I didn't catch your name," Nonie remained polite.

"Sorry, Mowbrie... Marcus Mowbrie."

Nonie looked at him in uncertainty. "What exactly do you want, Mr Mowbrie?"

"Just a concerned neighbour. Saw you were visiting; thought something might be amiss, in the spiritual sense, so to speak. I know a lot has gone on at that place..."

"No, nothing at all. Nothing that cannot be sorted out," Nonie replied. "If you don't mind, Mr Mowbrie, I really do need to be getting on my way. I have a ferry to catch." She began to wind the window up on her car. Mowbrie placed his hand on the glass, preventing her from winding up any further.

"Should I hear that there has been anything amiss, I won't be very happy, Ms Spangler," he hissed. "You see, we don't want any trouble around here. Folks like a peaceful life, if you get my meaning. They don't like interfering mediums on their patch. We don't want to hear of you discovering something amiss. Do you get my meaning?

Doesn't look good, not if the press were to hear of it. And, from all accounts, you don't need any more bad press, do you now?"

"Goodbye, Mr Mowbrie." Nonie forced his hand from the window and wound it shut. She accelerated away from him in a cloud of dust.

Mowbrie stood in the lane watching the car. He smiled to himself and walked back into the neighbouring field where his quad bike was parked out of sight.

□□□

"She was okay, I suppose. Nothing earth-shattering," Greta relayed her encounter with Nonie to Max on the phone. "I hate to say it, but you were right," she added and pursed her lips.

"At least she did pick up on the female. But she said something about two voices, talking over one another?" Max fiddled with the paperweight on his desk.

"Yes, but that's the only difference. I don't think I will bother with her any more. I seem to be picking up more information than she did." Greta sounded deflated.

"Well, as you know, I'll be back at the weekend and we can perhaps have another go at getting that treasure box out of the tunnel."

"We'll see." Greta didnt commit herself for fear of the consequences if they did remove the box. "I'm going back to mummy's now. Out for dinner tonight at the Smuggler's Hide."

□□□

"Well this is rather nice, isn't it? Just the three of us." Jeanne Standing had just been seated at their reserved table by Jonny Lucas.

"You chose a good time to come; before it gets really busy." Jonny placed three menus on the table. "Special tonight is Fruit de la Mar... seafood platter for two," he announced, clearly chuffed with his translation.

Greta smiled at Jonny's attempt at French and started to scan the menu. She wasn't feeling particularly hungry. She felt nervous of her previous encounters with Willow and she was bitterly disappointed that Nonie had not given her any new information. She tried to remain level headed.

"What are you going to have, darling?" Jeanne's voice was distant as Greta thought about Nonie.

She smiled. "Probably my favourite, scampi and chips."

"Ah, very good choice, love," Charles replied as he knocked his knife onto floor with the edge of his menu.

"Oh Charles, dear. You must be more *careful!*" Jeanne fussed as she bent down to retrieve the knife.

Greta glared at her mother.

"What did you just say?"

"That the father must be careful, why?" Jeanne looked surprised at Greta's reaction.

"Sorry, mummy. Nothing. I'm feeling quite tired; with all the work and stress at Greenacres. I didn't mean anything by it," she quickly apologised and looked down at the placemat, which was a carved piece of wood fashioned into the shape of the Isle of Wight. It had its fair share of ring marks stained on its surface. It felt sticky too.

"Well, I think the father and I will indulge in the Fruit de la Mar pour deux! Sounds scrummy!" Jeanne closed her menu and attracted Loo's attention from behind the bar, by madly flapping the menu high above her head. She had the habit of being to wrap most people around her little finger. Loo happily obliged and took the order.

"Any wine with your meal?" she sweetly suggested.

"We have a lovely Chablis that will complement the fish beautifully."

"We will be guided by your recommendation; thank you my dear," Jeanne loved the attention Loo was showing her. Greta continued to look to the table, dying of embarrassment. She felt her face redden. Poor Jeanne didn't realise Loo was very skilfully taking the rise.

"You're very quiet this evening, Greta?" Jeanne noticed Greta's ashen face.

"Sorry, not much fun am I? The injuries are playing up," she lied. In truth, she couldn't wait to escape.

"I'm just going to freshen up." She got up from the table and walked towards the Ladies. Jonny bypassed her passage.

"How are things at Greenacres? Everything all right?" Jonny quizzed. "Heard you had a visitor the other day."

"Wow, the news spreads like wildfire around here, doesn't it?" Greta didn't want to continue this particular awkward conversation.

"Heard it was a celebrity medium; the one off the TV. Having a spot of bother?" He carried on filling a pint glass with local Island ale. Loo, in the background, selected a bottle of chilled Chablis from the wine fridge, closed the door silently and listened intently.

"Yes, Nonie Spangler; she is… a friend of mine. We go back… years," Greta lied. "It is amazing how people put two and two together and get five, isn't it?"

"I thought it might be to do with the uh… tunnel," Jonny filled the pint glass and placed it onto a tray.

"The what?" Greta tried to sound incredulous.

"The tunnel. I'm surprised the vicar never mentioned it before he sold Greenacres to you. There's been talk of a tunnel linking this pub and Greenacres, for donkeys' years. Apparently it was used as a hide by smugglers; I'm talking years and years ago, centuries even. But no-one has ever proved it exists. The vicar had a few encounters, we are led to believe; he never said anything to anyone though. All speculation if you ask me. And there is a bit of a hint of a connection, isn't there, with the name of this place!"

"Hmm, yes. Sorry, I don't know anything about it. Good job the smugglers didn't know about it... if it did exist... otherwise they would have been queuing up for storage! Ha! Ha!" Greta cut the conversation with a fanatical burst of false laughter and looked towards the Ladies' room door.

"Sorry, nature calls!" She bobbed down as she spoke and dashed towards the toilet door.

Chapter Fifteen

"Greta, can you hear me?" Willow was trying to attract her attention. "I need to speak with you."

"Hmmmph?" Greta was in a deep sleep.

"I need to speak to you… now!" Willow was insistent.

"I'm listening," Greta mumbled.

"That woman that came to Greenacres today… she could quite clearly see me."

"What?" Greta tried to focus and engage her brain.

"That woman who came to the cottage, she could see me and she could see Evie as well. She didn't tell you everything."

Greta was still slumbering.

"What? Who's Evie?"

"Hello, Greta. I'm Evie," another female voice spoke through the darkness.

Greta was semi-conscious.

"Oh… okay, um, Evie. Are you with Willow?" Greta replied.

"Sometimes, yes, but other times we are in parallel worlds."

"Right," Greta continued, her eyes still closed. "So this woman, Nonie, saw you; did she see both of you?"

"Yes, but she didn't tell you everything." Willow repeated.

"What else should she have told me?" Greta propped her head on the pillow.

Willow paused. There was the faint sound of sobbing.

"Willow? You can't leave me dangling now!" she called out.

Evie spoke instead.

"Willow is too upset to say."

"About what? You must tell me!" Greta was getting worried.

"That woman also saw *him*."

"Who?" Greta snapped.

"*Him*… the one who murdered Willow. The man of the same name… who also murdered me!"

Greta sat bolt upright. She ran her fingers through her hair. She glanced at the clock on the bedside cabinet; it was 2.30am. She shook her head. This was becoming an habitual time to be woken up.

"Evie, are you there?" Greta called out into the darkness.

There was no reply. Greta was alone.

Greta plunged back on to her pillow in exasperation. Her mind raced back to Nonie's visit the day before. She sighed. It was too early to phone Max. He wouldn't appreciate a neurotic phone call in the middle of the night from his paranoid wife, talking about ghostly encounters; nor would Nonie. She dialled Sophie's number. At length it was answered by a croaky, sleep-wracked voice.

"Hmm… yeah? Who is this?"

"Sophie! It's Greta! Sorry hun; I know it's the middle of the night, but I had to ring you. I've had another spiritual encounter with Willow and another spirit, called Evie!"

"Wow! Are they having a ghost fest or something?"

Sophie muttered. She rubbed her eyes and tried to focus on the conversation. "What time is it?"

"Early. Listen; they are both saying they were murdered, by the same guy, with the *same* name. They haven't told me who, but I think it may shed some light on things. They're saying that Nonie Spangler could see them and this other bloke as well. What shall I do?"

"I think you should give Nonie a ring, not now; tell her what has happened and get her back over again. Sounds like between you all, you are unravelling a bit of a crime scene. It also sounds like you have just as much psychic power as Ms Spangler. Anyway, from what you said, she didn't spend much time with you, did she?"

"Oh, I don't know about that. But I think you're right, I'll get Nonie back over here and, you're right, she wasn't here any time at all," Greta agreed.

"Can I go back to sleep now?" Sophie sounded weary.

"Sorry, yes of course. I just needed to speak to someone; you did say, it was all right to phone... at any time." Greta apologised.

"I certainly did and it's okay. Night Greta. Sleep tight."

Greta lay back on the bed and drew the duvet to her chin. She closed her eyes and thought about Willow and Evie. Was she insane? Was she awake or dreaming? She couldn't decide. Suddenly she heard her name being called.

"Greta. Wake up! I need to talk to you!"

Greta groaned.

"Not again, surely. Now what?" she asked.

"It's the builder on the phone; it seems like there's a crisis at Greenacres!"

Greta opened her eyes to see her mother peering down at her. Holding the phone at arm's length, close to Greta's face.

"What's wrong?" Greta sat up in bed and took the phone. "Hello, yes. Really? Okay, give me half an hour, I'll be over."

She handed the phone back to her mother.

"Trouble in paradise, darling?" Jeanne enquired.

"Yes, something like that." Greta dragged herself out of bed and stumbled towards the bathroom.

"Shall I make breakfast?" Jeanne called out.

"Just toast and tea, thanks. I need to get over to Greenacres as soon as possible. Builders have found a problem," Greta replied. Then uttered under her breath. "From all accounts, a bloody big problem!"

As she arrived at the cottage, she could see the builders congregated outside in the garden, huddled together, deep in conversation. They dispersed as Greta approached them. The head builder looked pensive.

"Morning, Mrs Berkley; sorry to bother you so early, but we've got a bit of an issue. You see, we was trying to sort out how to do the feature on your well, when there was this almighty great banging noise coming from deep underground. Then, well, Jim here will tell you... go on Jim, say what you saw." The gaffer indicated for Jim to speak.

"Well, Missus, I was sat at the top of the 'ole then there was this loud noise, like thunder, underground. I could hear rocks and stuff falling; like there was an avalanche or something. Then when I turned round to speak to the gaffer, Mick's cup came flying at me and hit me right here!" he indicated with a stubby, hardworking, dirt encrusted finger, revealing an egg shaped swelling above his left eye.

"And then, when I tried to get up, something was holding me back down; like it didn't want me to leave. That was when the gaffer phoned you. Sorry, Missus, but I can't work in those sort of conditions; fair give me a fright, it did. My ticker can't take that sort of fright or assault! The boys here are worried about it too; don't like funny things happening. Especially as the cup broke and Mick hasn't got anything to drink his tea out of!"

The group of builders agreed by nodding and mumbling their thoughts.

"Sorry, Mrs Berkley, the boys aren't happy to work here any more. Until you can sort things out." The gaffer looked seriously at Greta.

"Then if the boys don't work, the boys don't get their pay!" Greta was fuming. "Are you trying to tell me there is something sinister in this cottage? Well, that is so absurd! I have never heard anything so preposterous!" She boomed and glared at each builder in turn.

"The boys are uncomfortable working in the kitchen. Everywhere else is fine, just there," the gaffer tried to reason.

"That is probably because everywhere else is virtually finished!" Greta said scornfully. "I repeat, no work; no pay. Take it or leave it. It's over to you boys! You haven't got much more to do here! You are virtually just finishing off!"

"That isn't fair, Mrs Berkley..." the gaffer began.

"Nor is your accusation that my cottage is haunted!" Greta fired back.

"Well, we're sorry, but we can't continue... but we expect to get our pay for what we have done today." The gaffer stood his ground.

"Okay, let's compromise. You carry on with the work and I will keep watch for any flying cups and bumps in the well and if we hear or see anything, then you can leave, immediately."

"But what about our pay?"

"You carry on and finish the work; then you will get your pay; stop and you don't, it's as simple as that!" Greta felt empowered. "Come on, everybody back to work. I will find Mick another cup, so he won't be without his tea. I will personally stand on guard at the well to ensure you will all be quite safe!"

She ushered the builders back into the cottage and into the kitchen. They reluctantly obliged, bickering amongst each other about who was going to work around the well opening.

"Chop! Chop! Kettle is about to be put on! Morning tea and coffee will shortly be served!" Greta clapped her hands loudly to encourage them back to their stations. "If you're lucky, you can have a biscuit too!"

The builders continued to work the entire day, incident free. They completed the task of building a circular dwarf wall around the well opening and made it safe by shoring up the walls in render. Greta sighed in relief as she watched them leave in convoy of white vans at 3pm. She checked her phone for messages. There was one from Nonie Spangler. *Sorry, only just got yr message from this am; will be on 3:15pm catamaran. Hope that's ok? Can you pick me up at 3.40pm? C u then. NS*

Greta punched the air; Nonie had agreed to a return visit. This time, Greta hoped it would be more productive than the previous. Greta closed her eyes and sighed; this was going to cost her a small fortune. Two ferry crossings in consecutive days, two investigations; another fifty pounds. Max wouldn't be very pleased. But Greta needed to get to the bottom of the mystery so that they could start their new life in the country in some sort of peace and, hopefully, tranquillity.

Chapter Sixteen

Nonie Spangler shuffled along the long line of dawdling passengers who were queuing to alight from the catamaran. Greta had texted her to say she would collect her from the Ryde Pier Head at around 3.45pm. She was leaning against her car when she saw Nonie tottering along carrying a bright red leather-look oversized handbag over her shoulder. She waved to attract Nonie's attention and Nonie duly returned the acknowledgement.

"Hello Greta! Sorry, but it's all been a bit of a rush. The train was held up for ages and I nearly missed my connection with the ferry." She opened the passenger door of Greta's car and collapsed on to the seat. "I thought I'd catch the train this time. The car ferry was so expensive!"

"Thanks for coming over again at such short notice. It seems like we have a situation at Greenacres. It even caused the builders to down tools; which I couldn't justify. Any excuse to have a break! I don't know! Oh, and is that handbag red for danger?" She indicated at Nonie's handbag. Nonie chose to ignore the comment and smirked.

"More activity of the paranormal variety, I take it?" Nonie wrestled with her seatbelt as Greta drove slowly up Ryde Pier, avoiding the commuters along the way and the speed ramps strategically placed upon the newly laid wooden boards. The Victorian buildings of Ryde town centre loomed closer.

"Yes. I wanted you to reinvestigate; to see what's going on. The builders were complaining of a collapse of masonry in the tunnel and noises too, coming from underground. One of them was allegedly hit by a flying cup, but I'm not convinced." She drove along the Esplanade through the town into the countryside.

"Well, I'll try my best to find out who or what it was… or is," Nonie smiled and held her handbag close to her as the car jolted over the bumpy road surface.

At length, they arrived at Greenacres. Greta turned off the ignition as Nonie looked startled.

"Oh!" she exclaimed. She was looking at the roof.

"Have you seen something?" Greta removed the key from the ignition and got out of the car.

"I'm not so sure." Nonie was still staring at the roof.

"Up there?" Greta pointed.

"I thought I saw something by the chimney." Nonie climbed out of the car, still clutching her handbag.

"Funny that," Greta replied. "Rev Oli was always staring at the roof; but he never said anything to us. Whatever it was, it seemed to have him in a complete trance."

"Hmmm." Nonie was not giving anything away.

"Come indoors and I'll show you the cup. You might be able to pick up something from that." Greta ushered Nonie inside to the kitchen and then came to an abrupt halt.

"What the hell is going on here?" she exclaimed and stormed over to the well. Nonie remained planted in the doorway. "I don't believe this!" Greta fumed.

Greta was standing by the feature wall of the well. She shook her head in disappointment.

"It is a complete mess! Look at this! It was fine when I left; now it's ruined!"

The newly built wall of the well had been smashed to pieces. Brick and masonry littered the floor and wet cement was spattered everywhere.

"This is really awful! Who would do such a thing?" Greta held her hand to her temple and shook her head.

Nonie joined her.

"So this has only happened since you left the cottage?"

"Yes; it can't be the builders; they wouldn't do such a terrible thing. They spent all day working on it; there is no way they would destroy their own handiwork. It must be an intruder."

"I take it you locked the door when you left to pick me up?" Nonie surmised.

"Course, yes. Max is a stickler for security and, having spent a lot of time living in London, that has fortunately rubbed off on me; I wouldn't dream of leaving the door unlocked." Greta walked around the circumference of the well. The top was exposed and a black gaping hole to the tunnel beneath glared up at her.

"Could this mean that someone or something gained entry from the tunnel?" Nonie asked.

"You tell me; that's is what you are here for, Nonie! Come on; what do you think?" Greta stood with her arms folded.

Nonie remained silent and closed her eyes. She nodded her head as though she was talking to someone. Greta stared at her. At length she spoke.

"Well?"

Nonie opened her eyes and blinked.

"From what I can tell from the spirit world, it was a human invader; not a spiritual one."

"Fantastic!" said Greta scornfully. "So now I have a vandal to deal with as well as the spirits! Bring it on..."

"Wait!" Nonie interrupted. "I am being given fresh information; from a female... she is saying it is the man."

"What man?" Greta placed her hands on her hips.

"The man; who has the same name..." Nonie was concentrating hard. Nonie closed her eyes again.

Greta looked at her.

"And what is the man's name?"

Nonie shook her head.

"She won't tell me; I think she wants me to work it out for myself... hold on! There is another voice... another female voice... she is warning me of the man... the man with the same name... wait! Don't go, I don't know what you mean... oh! She's gone."

"Damn it! Tell me exactly what they said." Greta paced around the kitchen narrowly avoiding tripping over a pile of bricks.

"There were two spirits; both talking over each other. One was a young girl, the other an older woman. They were warning me about this man... they kept saying he had the same name. I'm not sure what they meant; whether it is the same man or two different men. They weren't very forthcoming with the information. But they believe it to be a living being who had inflicted the damage to the wall and definitely not a spiritual one. Does that help you?" Nonie looked at Greta.

"Not really; you have basically told me everything I already knew. Didn't they give you any indication about what went on? What about the flying cup?"

"Sorry, they didn't. I'm feeling rather tired; do you mind if I take a step outside, to get some air?" Nonie walked towards the back door.

"No, of course not. Would you like some water?"

Greta offered.

"Yes, please." Nonie opened the door and stepped into the garden. She found a large millstone, promptly sat down and took a ferry timetable from her handbag and fanned her face. She looked very pale.

Greta, unsuccessful in her quest for a glass, carried a mug of water out to Nonie who took a sip along with a small pink tablet.

"Sorry it's in a mug, we haven't brought any glasses over yet. Are you feeling okay?" Greta was concerned. She sat alongside Nonie who remained pale.

"Just a little faint, dear," she replied and sipped at the water. She looked up to the chimney once more. "It saps my energy; it's such a nuisance."

"Tell me; what did you see up there?" Greta knew Nonie was hiding something from her.

Nonie took a deep breath.

"I… um, think I saw a shadow of a figure, maybe a man; I certainly saw a raised hand." She took a slug of water with another tablet and made a face as she swallowed. "He was stood very defiant; like he was guarding the cottage. Then, when we were in the kitchen, he appeared by the well. He was very angry; said he didn't want us there; sorry, Greta. I haven't been much help."

"Did he say who he was?" Greta probed.

"No, no, he didn't," Nonie replied. She wiped her mouth with a crumpled tissue she had retrieved from her handbag.

"Do you know who he might be?" Greta continued.

"Sorry, no. But he appears to be a very unhappy, restless spirit; I didn't want to push him; spirits like these can be extremely dangerous if provoked. I kept my distance from him. One thing is for sure though…"

"Yes?" Greta held her breath.

"Greenacres will be a fantastic place to live, once you have finished the renovations!" Nonie got up from the millstone and handed Greta her empty mug. "Could I use your loo, please?"

Deflated, Greta nodded in silence.

"First door on left up the stairs. Mind the floor as you go. It might still be tacky from the stain."

"Thank you, dear." Nonie disappeared back into the cottage.

Greta's phone vibrated. It was a message from Max.

Hi, how are things at Greenacres? it read.

Greta returned her message.

Couldn't be better x

She decided not to update Max on the current catastrophe. She sighed as she thought about Nonie. She was having serious doubts about her capabilities as a medium. She was concerned that if Nonie were telling the truth, how would she get rid of the evil male spirit? She decided to tackle Nonie head on when she saw her appear at the back door.

"What is the next course of action, Nonie?" She stood up from her cold stone seat.

"Well, dear. There isn't anything more I can do for now." Nonie fumbled in her handbag.

"What do you mean? Nothing more? I want to be rid of this evil spirit! I don't want to be living under the same roof as him! You *must* be able to do *something*!" she was incredulous at Nonie's dismissal.

"He is rather too much for me and my capabilities, Greta. He is taking all my energy," Nonie replied, looking up at the roof.

"I am paying you to be capable, Nonie. That is what you are here for! Honestly, the works here cannot progress until we have this spirit moved out of the cottage. I can't have the builders making any further excuses to stop working; not at this crucial stage. Or for any more interruptions to the renovations. I need you to help me, please!"

Nonie nodded in silence. She paused before she spoke.

"I don't think I can be of any further help, dear. Not today, I am very weak. Perhaps another time."

"You are kidding, aren't you? I want answers; I don't want to wait any longer. Besides, it's getting very expensive!" Greta stood firm.

Nonie shook her head.

"Sorry, Greta. I can't do any more here. Do you mind taking me back to the ferry?"

"I don't believe it! In fact, I am beginning to think that the newspapers were right about you!"

"What are you saying, dear?" Nonie looked taken aback.

"That you are a fake! And that all your shows are staged and paying members of the public are being duped by your inability to communicate with the spirit world. I'm right, aren't I?" Greta demanded.

Nonie looked shocked. She thought for a while and then softly spoke.

"Have you ever heard of someone called Barnabas?"

Greta shook her head.

"Barnabas? Barnabas who?"

Nonie swallowed and looked up at the roof. "Just Barnabas."

Greta thought for a moment.

"No, sorry. I've not heard of a Barnabas. Do you have another name? Surname or first name?"

"Barnabas is the name I have been given. I didn't want to say anything until I was quite sure. But, in the circumstances and to prove my worth, I felt compelled to tell you," Nonie replied. She was still reeling from Greta's verbal attack.

"Okay. So we have a name. That's a start, isn't it? Anything else?" Greta continued.

"One more name that I've been given… it could be a name or it could be a tree…"

"Is it Willow, by any chance?" Greta asked impatiently.

"Yes, dear. Funnily enough, it is," Nonie replied. She looked distant.

"Now we are getting somewhere. I have definitely heard of Willow. In fact, I have had a conversation or two with Willow, in the early hours. And of all places at my parents' home!"

Nonie nodded.

"Hmm. Willow. Pretty name; pretty girl. She isn't very old, what a terrible shame. Spirits don't always stay in one place. They do travel about, particularly if they want to communicate with you. She obviously felt a strong need to contact you, wherever you might be."

Greta gritted her teeth. She was becoming increasingly frustrated with Nonie and her communication skills.

"What was a shame?"

Nonie looked sad.

"That she died so young."

"Right. So we have established Willow died young and a man called Barnabas is in my kitchen wrecking my newly built well wall. What is the connection between them?"

Nonie had closed her eyes once more and was concentrating very hard.

"Hello, Evie. Right… I will." Nonie was in a trance.

Greta pursed her lips. She was irritated that she had to bully Nonie into doing what she was paid to do. The threat of being a fake and not paying her had spurred her into a delayed reaction. Now she was finally getting somewhere. She felt Nonie was conning her and making excuses to come back again, to retrieve a further fee.

"What has Evie told you?" Greta cut to the chase.

"Something quite disturbing, dear," Nonie replied, her eyes still tightly shut.

"Tell me something new!" Greta mumbled.

"Okay, I will," Nonie replied. "Willow told me that she was murdered. Here at Greenacres. This Barnabas, was involved. In fact, Barnabas was the perpetrator."

Greta nodded. "So she was telling the truth, definitely murdered?" she whispered. "And this Barnabas person murdered Willow?"

"Yes, dear. He apparently strangled her. That's what she informed me. She is very scared." Nonie looked up to the window once more.

"What of? What's she scared of?" Greta nervously asked.

"Scared that he might… that he might do it again," Nonie responded.

"What do you mean? That's impossible, he can't kill her again, can he? When was Willow murdered? Can she give you any sort of date or timescale?" Greta gripped Nonie's arm.

"Yes, she gave me a date… 1701. In the winter of 1701. It was cold; snow was lying thickly on the ground. She remembers the cold; so cold… his hands gripping hard around her neck; her breath, shallow… fighting for breath. The cold biting, his hands tightening around her neck, his hands were cold… then nothing…"

"How terrible!" Greta was shocked to think of a murder happening in such a tranquil location. "What about Evie? What happened to Evie? Did she die here too?"

Nonie paused then nodded her head solemnly.

"Yes, dear. She died here too. She died in the garden."

"Oh no; what happened to her? Did she have a heart attack?" Greta knowingly played along.

"No, dear. I'm sorry to say that she too was murdered."

Greta raised her eyebrows. "Great! So I have a cottage steeped in a murderous past! Aren't I lucky?"

"Not so long ago, it happened within the last few years. It was a man with the same name... he pushed her... pushed her so hard she couldn't get up again... the ground was wet against her skin... he knelt over her, where she lay, holding her down... holding his hand over her nose and mouth... he had cold, clammy hands..."

"What do you mean, by a man with the same name? Surely they weren't both called Barnabas; that would be too much of a coincidence! Anyway, there is a couple of hundred years between them!" Greta's mind raced.

"Both had the same name, dear. That is what Evie is telling me. Both had the same *surname*!"

Greta looked alarmed. She jumped as her phone began to ring. She pressed the ignore button.

"What's the surname?"

Nonie didn't answer immediately. She was in spiritual communication again. She eventually spoke.

"Sorry, dear. They've gone. I can't get any more information from them."

Nonie flopped back on to the millstone, gasping with exhaustion. Greta was speechless. She held her hand to her head and ran her fingers through her hair. She got up and paced around the garden.

"Are you sure they didn't give you any clues as to what the name was?" she spoke at length.

"No, dear. They have both gone now. I cannot raise them."

Greta thought for a moment.

"Nonie, would you mind staying overnight? Perhaps we can continue with this investigation tomorrow? How would you feel about that? How is your diary fixed?"

Nonie considered.

"I would love to, dear, provided I can get some rest. My diary is free for the next few days. I think we have a mystery on our hands that needs to be solved."

"I can offer you a room at my mother's house. I just need to make a phone call to confirm things with her," Greta replied.

"That would be fine, dear. I am feeling rather shattered now and am in need of a lie down." Nonie looked flushed.

"You've certainly proved one thing," Greta smiled.

"What's that, dear?"

"You certainly aren't a fake!"

Chapter Seventeen

Greta turned the key in the car's ignition as Nonie again wrestled with her seatbelt and her large, red handbag. They drove slowly back up the unmade lane. A flock of birds circled around the cottage high in the air; crows cawed in the tops of the ash trees that lined the garden at Greenacres. Pigeons fought for space in amongst the branches as dusk was beginning to fall. The sky was turning to aubergine with flames of red stripes, tinged with pink. The trees in the distance were grey against the failing light.

"Mummy is looking forward to meeting you, Nonie. I found out recently that she is quite keen on paranormal topics. I expect she'll want to quiz you a bit."

Nonie smiled. "Most people do want to pick my brain, when they find out what I do. Curiosity mainly."

"Right."

They hadn't seen the dark figure crouching low down and close to the hedgerow along the lane. As the car passed by, it suddenly sprang into life and made a dash towards the cottage. The figure was of a man, dressed in black with an athletic physique as he tore off at a sprint to the back of Greenacres and into the garden. Stopping to catch his breath, he pulled out a mobile phone and dialled a number. Swallowing to compose himself, he spoke.

"Yeah, I'm here. Now what?" He waited as he was given an instruction. "Seriously? You're not right in the head, mate. Surely not?" he questioned his task that he had been instructed to complete. "I might be fit and healthy, but that's just outrageous!" He ended the call abruptly and swore to himself. Clearly, he was not happy with what he had been told to do. He shook his head and made another call.

"Yeah, it's me. Look, I can't see you tonight. Something has come up. No, not sure. I'll ring you. Bye."

The man paced around the garden for a time, muttering to himself in the gathering darkness. He lit a cigarette and took a long, deep draw, so the amber embers were quite prominent against the sky. He pulled a small metal hip flask from his coat pocket and took a swig from it. He made a face as the alcohol trickled down his throat. He paced around the garden for a few minutes and then turned on his heel. He picked up a large stone from the ground and threw it purposefully at the kitchen window. The impact was minimal as the glass fractured into a million pieces, however it held its place within its UPVC frame. The man used his elbow to clear away spent shards, which scattered on to the floor. He reached inside and turned the handle and the frame opened easily.

Once inside, the man held a torch to the entrance to the well and pulled out his phone. He made another call. He spoke in a hushed whisper.

"I'm in; now what?" He awaited further instruction. "Is that possible?" he questioned. "You're having a joke... yeah, right!"

He leaned over the hole in the floor where the pile of bricks lay scattered and shone the torch down inside. "It's a long way down; where? Are you sure?" He wildly looked around for a ladder. "There isn't one; they must have taken it." He added, "I don't know, she's only just left. Okay, I'll try… *I said*, I'll try, I can't promise anything! You don't even know what's down there!"

He ended the call and shone the torch around the kitchen. The builders had taken the ladder with them. The man, in desperation, peered down the entrance to the hole. As he was leaning over, deciding whether to jump, a shadowy male figure, which was stood behind him, rose up and swiftly pushed with such force the man instantly disappeared down the hole.

"Erghhhhhh!" His voice disappeared into the well as he fell. He landed with a smack on the ground and laid still. He was still holding the torch as he tried to move.

"Argh!" he yelped as a sharp pain travelled up from his ankle. "Shit!" His phone rang simultaneously.

"Yeah? No, I'm *not* all right. I don't know what happened. One minute I was at the top, and for some reason, it felt like something pushed me. I fell down it. I've done something to my bloody ankle. It is killing me! I don't know! I haven't tried to move it."

He tried to get up. The pain from his ankle was intense. He had been immobilised. "Sorry mate, no can do. I have done some serious damage to it. I need help!" he panted as the pain from his ankle made him close his eyes in agony. "I think I've broken it! I can't feel my toes. I'm in a bad way! You need to get me out of here, now! You and your hare-brained ideas… you'd better had get me out; I'm telling you, I'm not staying here till they get back! What? You have got to be kidding me!" He was incredulous. "Hello? Hello? Well, fuck you then!" He threw the phone across the ground and it disappeared into a mass of mud and cobwebs.

Chapter Eighteen

"Delighted to meet you, Ms Spangler!" Jeanne held out her hand to Nonie. "Do come in. I am Jeanne and this is my husband, Charles." She indicated to Charles who was loitering in the doorway staring at her in a very dubious way.

Nonie smiled and shook his hand.

"I will show you to your room, dear." Jeanne fussed Nonie towards the staircase and indicated for her to follow.

"What a charming house, Mrs Standing." Nonie slowly climbed the stairs and gazed at the paintings adorning the walls as she went.

"Oh! Call me Jeanne, please!" Jeanne cooed. She reached the landing and pointed to a door. "Here is your room, dear. Freshen up and come down for a cup of tea. I will be serving it in the drawing room!"

"Thank you. But if it's all the same with you, I will have a lie down. I'm feeling rather weak." Nonie sank down on to the bed and sighed.

"Oh, oh, that's such a shame," Jeanne looked disappointed but overcame it with a smile. She took the hint to leave. She quietly closed the bedroom door behind her.

Greta was in the living room with her father. Jeanne spoke in a whisper.

"Are you going to tell me what's going on? Do you have psychic problems at Greenacres?"

"You could say that," Greta smiled weakly.

"And... ?" Jeanne was in suspense. She folded her arms and clutched her sides tightly.

"I think Greenacres is haunted," Greta announced.

"Oh no! My dear girl!" Jeanne spluttered. "Does Maxim know?"

Greta nodded. "Yes. But he's so sceptical. He thinks he may have heard or seen something. But he isn't convinced. I told him I thought it was haunted and managed to talk him around to getting Nonie to investigate."

Jeanne was perversely intrigued. Her eyes were wide with unmistakable excitement. "Has she found anything?"

"Yes, it is unravelling to be a bit of a crime scene; historically; not in recent times."

"How fascinating!" Jeanne perched on the edge of Charles's armchair. "How romantic!"

"I wouldn't say it is romantic, mummy. Unnerving is more the case and a pain in the bum."

"Have *you* seen anything untoward?" Jeanne probed.

"Hmmm, possibly. But I need to know for sure; from Nonie."

Jeanne paused before she eventually spoke.

"But isn't she a fake, dear? A phoney?"

"That's what I need to establish. I have an inkling of what is going on at Greenacres myself. But I need to hear it and have it confirmed from someone independently."

"Good idea, darling!"

"Load of old codswallop, if you ask me, my girl!" Charles dared to air his point of view. He was immediately shot down in flames by Greta.

"So you are an expert on the paranormal now then, are you?" Greta shrieked.

Charles was alarmed at Greta's outburst.

"Uh… no, but honestly love, ghosts?"

Greta glared at him.

"Dad, you don't know anything!" She got up and stormed out of the room. Jeanne sighed and stared at her husband. She slowly clapped her hands together in a sarcastic applause.

"Well done, dear! Always one to put your size nines in it!" She left Charles alone. He remained defiant, staring into open space. His lips were in a military pout, almost covering the lower part of his nose.

Greta was stood in the kitchen. She was furious. Jeanne placed a sympathetic hand on her shoulder.

"Don't listen to him, dear. He has no idea what he's talking about."

"Too right, he doesn't know! Why is he so quick to scorn it?" Greta sniffed.

"It's because he's scared, darling. Scared of what might be. Nothing more. He's a silly old fool."

Greta blew her nose noisily into a piece of kitchen paper. Jeanne retrieved a tissue and handed it as a replacement to Greta, clearly concerned about her daughter using incorrect paper.

"I don't want Greenacres to be suffering. I want it to be free from anything evil that's lurking there. It isn't fair! Why didn't the Rev Oli tell us? Why?" she snivelled from behind her tissue.

"I must admit that it wasn't very clever missing out the fact that Greenacres might have a spiritual lodger."

"Perhaps he genuinely didn't know about it. But then, he *must* have known!" Greta tried to reason. "He knew about the deaths, of the two women, one of them was his tenant! He must know about everything that happened there!"

"Being a man of the cloth, he probably didn't want to

cause a stir. Religious people are very wary of supernatural things, aren't they? They don't believe in ghosts, but they do cherish the fact there is an afterlife," Jeanne tried to reassure Greta.

"Convenient, wouldn't you say?" Greta wiped her corner of her eyes with the tissue.

"Have you thought about asking him for some more information?" Jeanne asked.

"No, not until now. Now I want to quiz him about absolutely everything."

"I suggest you get some rest, darling. Perhaps phone the Reverend later and arrange to meet with him?"

Greta distantly nodded. "Okay."

"I'll make some tea and take a cup up to Nonie. She wanted to have a rest."

"I'll go and make my peace with the father." Greta raised her eyebrows and walked into the drawing room.

Charles was staring into the fireplace. He glanced at Greta and resumed his defiant, stubborn look.

"You don't need to look like that any more, dad. I'm sorry for yelling at you. You are entitled to your own opinion and I respect that. I just need answers, that's all. And if I am wrong about Greenacres, and I sincerely hope that I am, then that will be the end of it. Nothing more will be said about it. Will you forgive me?"

Charles sniffed in an offish fashion and eventually grumbled.

"Yes, as long as you don't dwell on things. When people die, that's it; they are gone... forever! Some people believe there's a paradise; a heaven, when death occurs. I'm afraid I'm not one of them. Probably because my father didn't believe and he instilled the same into me, as a young boy. Old habits die hard, my dear. Didn't mean anything by it." He indicated for Greta to sit beside him on the rug.

She obediently sat at his feet, staring into the embers of the fire. Charles stroked her hair.

"It's not like you to stand up for yourself, dad." Greta smiled as she spoke.

"No. Most of the time I tend to humour your mother. She loves to get her own way, so why should I stand in her way? It's much easier to agree with her. But this; well, it's something I feel *very* strongly about. Nothing more; it's nothing against you. But I'm not keen on having that medium thingy... person in our house. Makes me feel like she is taking the rise; like she is trying to pretend she is something that she isn't. Charlatan, I think, is the best word to describe her." Charles continued to stroke Greta's hair.

"Like Lawrence of Arabia?" She looked up at Charles.

"Exactly... complete charlatan!" He smiled and reached over to place another log of wood on the dying embers of the fire.

Chapter Nineteen

The following morning dawned grey and overcast. There was a haze of mist over the ground, like a carpet of smoky incandescence. As Greta and Nonie drove down the track towards Greenacres, it couldn't have looked more sinister or spooky. The cottage walls protruded through the mist in patches, making the whole place appear as though it was floating off the ground. Greta gritted her teeth. She was determined to solve more of the mystery that Greenacres held. She looked across at Nonie, who had her eyes tightly closed.

"Are you sensing something already, Nonie?" Greta was concerned.

"No, dear. I'm just feeling a bit queasy. Probably from the car ride." Nonie opened her eyes. She shuffled through her handbag and retrieved a bottle of smelling salts. She removed the lid and took a deep breath. "That's better." She made a face as the smelling salts, which, Greta noticed, were exceptionally potent. "I'll be fine... urgh!" she spluttered.

"Well, we're here." Greta parked the car around the side of the cottage. She noticed the lack of builders' vans in the driveway. Greenacres was silent.

"Come on Nonie, we have work to do." She encouraged Nonie to get out of the car.

Clutching a set of keys, Greta sauntered to the back door and turned the lock. As she opened the door, she stopped. She noticed something wasn't right with the kitchen window and wandered over to take a look. She yelled in dismay.

"I don't believe it! Look, the window has been smashed! Oh no!"

She dashed back to the door and threw it open. As she did so, she reached for her phone and dialled Max's number. It went to voicemail. She didn't leave a message. As she walked into the house, she was hit by an invisible force that threw her on to the back foot. She staggered to remain upright. She shook her head and blinked.

"Christ! It absolutely stinks inside. It smells like a sewer! Positively foul!" She looked over to Nonie, who was staring at the roof. "Come on, Nonie, help me. We need to get inside, but you will need to put something over your nose and mouth. It reeks!"

"Just as I thought," Nonie muttered, shaking her head.

"What?" Greta handed Nonie a cotton scarf. "Here, take this, you'll need it."

"I don't know. I am sensing it's his way of trying to prevent you from going inside. A smokescreen... or something."

"More like shit screen! Sorry, I don't mean to be coarse, but it really does smell like it!" Greta draped her scarf across her nose. She held her breath and stepped inside the kitchen. She closed her eyes and made face.

"Oh! It's coming from the well. Now, why doesn't that surprise me?"

Determined not to be defeated by whatever barriers

threatened her, Greta strode forwards into the kitchen.

"Don't think you've won this bout, matey; it is only just beginning!" she shouted aloud in hope that something might hear her.

Nonie was a little more reserved in her entrance into the kitchen. She held her scarf tightly across her nose and slowly surveyed the room. She caught a glimpse of a shadow near the entrance to the well and focused on it. She waved in silence to get Greta's attention.

"Over there!" Nonie whispered and indicated by frantic pointing and waving of her hand. "I have seen something over there!"

"What?" Greta whispered back. She looked puzzled. "Why are we whispering?"

"I don't know. I saw something over there!" Nonie repeated and waved at the direction of the well.

"Was it him? Was it this *Barnabas* person?" Greta was getting impatient.

Nonie was silent. She shook her head. "I couldn't tell if it was him or not. It was a black shadowy figure, lurking near the well entrance. I think this issue with the smell is his way of trying to put us off."

"Well it will take more than that to put me off. If it were a plague of…" she shuddered, "… urgh, spiders, wow, I said it! Well then, it might have more of an effect! Perish the thought. It has an aroma of death about it!"

"Don't!" Nonie hissed.

"What?" Greta frowned.

"Think of spiders, cos if he is the type of spirit I think he is, with pure evil on his mind, it might just be that he confronts you with… your own worst fear. Clear your mind! Now! Quickly!"

"Okay, I am trying to," Greta panicked and looked wildly around her. "It's okay, I've not seen any of them yet."

"Clear, your, mind!" Nonie sounded strange. Her voice had changed. The tone of it sounded deep and sinister.

"Do it now… clear your mind… urgh!" She fell backwards against a granite work surface and struggled to stay on her feet. "Don't do that! Don't you dare do that to me!" she shouted into the air. She clung to the edge of the work surface. "How dare you! How dare you!" She regained her balance and stood defiantly in the centre of the room.

"Nonie! Are you all right?" Greta was spooked at Nonie's action.

"Yes, I'm just dandy!" she replied, with her arms folded. "Is that the best you can do? You know you cannot win! You cannot win this!" She paced slowly around the kitchen.

A groan from below in the well stopped her.

"What the hell was that?" Greta screamed and looked across at Nonie who was holding on to her side, wincing in pain.

"I don't know, what was what?"

"There was a noise, from the well; a groan. Listen!"

"Ergh, heeeelp me… !" the voice wailed from below. "I need… heeelp!"

"It's a voice! Someone is in the well! Is it that Barnabas bloke?" Greta shrieked.

Nonie shuffled to where Greta was stood. She listened at the entrance.

"I can't hear anything. But I am more concerned about what is behind you!" she slowly raised her finger and pointed to the wall. Greta froze and whispered.

"What? You're scaring me, Nonie! What is it?"

Nonie was holding her own conversation.

"Is that right? Oh do you now? Well, aren't you the big man? Don't think you can do the same to us. You can't hurt either of us. You aren't living; you are a spirit, you are dead. You are not of this world. In fact, you are nobody! Nobody wanted you in life, did they? And now, nobody wants you in the spirit world. I'm right, aren't I? You are a menace, as you were in this world. A complete menace that only survived by preying on other people and their property. That's what you did, didn't you? Prey on other people. Prey on women. Poor, defenceless women; it wasn't just Willow, was it? Who else did you prey on? Who else did you bully? Who else did you... murder... urgh!"

"For god's sake! Someone help me!" the weak voice called from the well floor.

Nonie fell to the floor like a stone. The contents of her handbag spilled on to the floor. She writhed on the floor, tossing from one side to the other, moving away from an invisible force that appeared to be above her. She inched her way over the flagstone floor by pushing her feet underneath her and struggling to escape for all she was worth. Greta was in shock. She couldn't comprehend what was happening. She stood in the kitchen with her hands held tightly over her ears.

"Nonie!" she screamed. "Can you hear me? Do you need help?"

"He's right above me, Greta. It's Barnabas! He's stood over me. He is trying to get his hands... oh, hand; he has a hook. He only has one hand! He's trying to get it around my neck! Get help. Summon the Reverend! Get him over here now!" she gasped as she closed her eyes. She choked as she spoke. "He... is trying to... strangle me... help... help!"

Greta's mind raced back to the encounter in the drawing room. "He only has one hand..." Realisation hit her. The severed hand! She focussed her mind and grabbed her mobile phone. The signal had died. She ran outside and a faint signal appeared on the screen. She dialled the Rev Oli. As she did so, she peered through the kitchen window and could see Nonie still writhing on the floor, shouting obscenities to what appeared to be thin air.

"Er, hello? Rev Oli? Yes, it's Greta Berkley. Yes, yes, I'm fine. Look, I need your help! We need your help. Now! It's very, very urgent!"

"Why Gretel, you sound so distressed! What in heaven's name is the matter?" Rev Oli nervously asked.

"There is no time to explain! We have a problem, or maybe several problems, at Greenacres. We need your help in the professional sense. Please hurry! And can you please bring some holy water with you. I think we may be in dire need of it!"

Greta abruptly ended the call. Rev Oli stared at the phone, replaced the receiver on its cradle and ambled towards the door of the vicarage.

Greta dashed back into the kitchen. Nonie was lying still on the floor.

"Oh no! Nonie! Can you hear me?" Greta dropped to the floor beside Nonie and listened for her breathing.

Nonie was motionless. Her breathing was very shallow.

"Nonie! Speak to me!" Greta shook the lifeless body. "Come on! Don't let him defeat you! He must not defeat you!"

Nonie's eyes flickered for an instant. She blinked and drew breath. She pointed to her inhaler that was strewn across the floor.

"There… fetch it… over there!" she whimpered.

Greta looked across the room and lunged for the inhaler. She passed it to Nonie and puffed some blasts into her mouth.

Nonie spluttered and started choking.

"More?" Greta shrieked.

Nonie nodded without speaking. Again, Greta puffed the inhaler into Nonie's mouth. She paused.

"Is that enough?" She glanced at Nonie, whose eyes were flickering.

"Yes," Nonie whispered. "Enough... enough..."

"Are you okay?" Greta checked Nonie's pulse. It was very rapid.

Nonie nodded.

"I will be; just give me a minute or two." She coughed and cleared her throat. "He was pushing so hard on my chest, the air was literally being squeezed out of me. He is very powerful, so very powerful. He nearly throttled me to death."

"I know, I could see it; I mean, I could tell. I couldn't see him. I felt so helpless. I really did. I couldn't help you. But I've spoken to the Reverend. He is coming over right away. Hopefully, if you are up to it and he is as well, between you, you can get rid of this Barnabas."

"Yes, dear. That would be the plan. When will the Reverend be here?" Nonie sat up and reached over for her handbag. She began to refill it with the contents that were scattered across the floor. Her breathing was still irregular.

"He didn't say; but I said it was very urgent... what's that?" Greta got up off the floor as she heard a car door slam. It was Rev Oli.

"Gretel, my dear!" he held out his hands to Greta as he rushed through the doorway. He clasped hold of her hands in a reverential fashion.

"Oh, Rev Oli. We are in desperate need of you. We have a problem," Greta walked the Rev into the kitchen. "This is Nonie Spangler. She is a spiritual medium. She's here to help me solve a few problems that Greenacres appears to have. But she cannot do it alone. She has found a troublesome spirit, who is intent on causing harm. Can you please help us, Rev?" Greta looked deeply into Rev Oli's eyes.

"Well, good day to you Miss Spangler. I cannot say that our paths have ever crossed. Please tell me what is happening here."

"Oh Reverend," Nonie slowly rose to her feet and held out her hand. It was shaken limply by Rev Oli. "I am usually quite capable of dealing in such situations with spirits; but I have never encountered such a powerful one as this. I am hoping with your help, we can move this gentleman out of Greenacres for good. Are you willing to help?"

Rev Oli was silent. He looked perturbed. He scratched his head and frowned.

"What is this spirit you have discovered?"

"His name is Barnabas. He…" Nonie stopped dead in her tracks. Rev Oli had turned very pale. He held his hand to his head and spun around. "What?" he yelled in a most out of character fashion.

"What did you say he was called?" he reiterated.

"Uh, Barnabas. But I don't have a surname. I can't seem to reach any conclusion regarding a surname." Nonie puzzled and picked up her handbag from the floor.

"No, no, you must be mistaken. Truly mistaken." Rev Oli paced around the kitchen, still holding his hand to his head. His face remained pale. The colour had completely drained from him.

"I have been informed by two different sources and they both say the same name. Barnabas. The sources also tell me that he has the same surname. But I can't fathom out what they actually mean."

Rev Oli was silent. He paced around the kitchen, avoiding the well. At length, he spoke.

"I think I can answer that question. In fact, I am sure

I can. This Barnabas person is someone that I am unfortunately aware of. However, I wish I wasn't. His name has plagued me for years. On deeds to Greenacres, I saw the name. In idle chitchat, I hear his name; in my deepest fears, I know of his name. He is, or rather, he was, in life, Barnabas Mowbrie... heaven help me for saying that name." Rev Oli broke off and stood at the window gazing into the garden.

Nonie and Greta stood in silence, hardly daring to take in what the Rev had just said. Greta shook her head.

"Of the same name. He has the same name..." She looked at the Reverend. "Does this mean... can this mean, that we have a neighbour who is a relation of Barnabas Mowbrie?"

Rev Oli nodded.

"I am afraid so, Gretel. I am so sorry."

"And you knew about this? About this Barnabas person?" Greta was feeling anger building up inside.

Rev Oli nodded.

"Yes, I am aware of Barnabas, but not of all his ancestral history. I am aware he was a smuggler who lived at Greenacres, in the 1700s. There is talk that the cottage was linked with the Smuggler's Hide pub and that Barnabas and his accomplices dug a tunnel between the two properties to store smuggled goods... contraband, and travel unseen along it, out of sight of the customs men. I am not sure what he smuggled, but I can only assume it was the usual smuggling booty - alcohol and tobacco."

"So you knew of his connection with Greenacres?" Greta snapped.

"Yes, my dear. I'm afraid I did know."

"Did you know what happened to him? How he died?"

Rev Oli shook his head.

"No. Only that he smuggled contraband and stored it

here, or possibly underground. I never knew of his demise. I don't know if anyone is aware. It comes up for discussion every now and then in idle gossip but any rumour is instantly quashed by Mr Marcus Mowbrie."

"Funny that, isn't it." Greta walked away and thrust her hands into her pockets. "I wonder *why* Marcus Mowbrie covered up any rumours? I wonder how much he has to hide?"

"I don't really wish to talk about that man," Rev Oli shuddered. His shoulders quaked as he spoke. "He's not a particularly nice person. He is, has been very... threatening."

"I'm not surprised, judging by the way his ancestor behaved. So now we know why he was so desperate to buy Greenacres. Because it was the family home. Why have you prevented him from doing so? Don't you fear for your life, Rev Oli? Don't you go to bed some nights and wonder if you will ever wake up?"

"Greta! That's enough!" Nonie shrieked.

"No, Nonie, it isn't! I am sickened by the fact that Rev Oli here LIED to us, to Max and to me. He knew perfectly well what had happened here. He decided to omit that from the sales details. What else did you conveniently forget to tell us, Reverend? Do tell us, I am dying to know!" Greta scoffed.

"My dear... Gretel..." Rev Oli began.

"Just one more thing!" Greta roared. "It is Greta! Not Gretel, Greta! If you are going to address me, then *please* get my name correct! G, R, E, T, A! Greta! I am not something out of a nursery rhyme or fable. Unlike your version of events! Do you understand?"

Rev Oli closed his eyes. He didn't speak. Greta looked at Nonie, who was horrified. She took Greta to one side and held her arm.

"You shouldn't speak to a man of the cloth like that, Greta. It is very disrespectful. You should apologise to him, now!"

Greta shrugged off Nonie's grasp on her arm.

"Don't you think *he* should apologise to us, for selling us a property that is involved in murder and plagued by the dead? Come on Nonie, I don't think I should be the one apologising! He should be on his knees for this! He knew all along about this Barnabas character. He probably couldn't believe his luck when Max and I were desperate to buy this place. He was probably doing cartwheels down the aisle! What?"

Nonie pointed at the Reverend who had keeled over by the well. He looked as if he had been punched in the stomach.

"So what? He is probably looking for God!" Greta sneered and walked over to where Rev Oli was poised.

"What can you see? Is it Barnabas or the devil?"

Rev Oli held on to his side. He was breathing strangely.

"I think we have another encounter with Barnabas about to start," Nonie indicated towards the well.

There was a strange light flashing on and off at the bottom of the well. It was intermittent and very bright. Rev Oli held on to the remaining bricks of the well wall and reached inside his jacket pocket. He drew out a small bottle of water and a wooden cross. Nonie reached out and steadied him as he stood upright and clasped a small black bible in his other hand. He passed the bottle of water to Greta.

"Unscrew this for me, Greta. Hold it in front of me."

"Please help me…" the voice from the passage below croaked.

He thumbed through the bible until he reached a marked page and began reciting from the Book of John.

Holding the cross at arm's length into the mouth of the well, he continued to speak in a monotone voice.

"…but the will of him that sent me. And this is the Father's will which hath sent me, that of which he hath given me…."

Within seconds, Rev Oli was hurled backwards by an unseen force. He was thrown to the ground and his head hit against the wall. He lay crumpled in a corner of the kitchen, his head bowed forwards. He still held on to the cross and gradually lifted his arm with the cross defiantly in his hand. He continued to mutter from the Book of John.

"Greta! Unscrew the bottle. When the Reverend finishes speaking, flick it into the direction of the well. Not all of it, just a few drops. We don't want to waste any." Greta looked at the bottle and did as she was asked. Rev Oli was still muttering.

"Okay, when I say so, flick the water over the well!" Nonie was standing by the side of Greta and looking at Rev Oli at the same time.

"Do it NOW!" she yelled.

Greta flicked the bottle for all she was worth. As the water hit the sides of the well, it hissed and spat as though it was boiling.

"He's there; Barnabas is down there!" Nonie pointed to the well. "Do it again, Greta! Again!" she urged.

Greta flicked more water into the well and again it fizzled in retaliation.

"Stop throwing water over me! Just get me out of here!" a voice squeaked from beneath the ground.

"Okay, I am getting a message from Willow…"

"What?" Greta squeaked.

"Wait?" Nonie was silent. "Okay, right. She is telling me that Barnabas is refusing to go. That there is something else in the tunnel."

"What? You don't say!" Greta's sarcasm returned.

"Yes. He is threatening Willow and Evie again. He... wait... he... oh, no..." Nonie froze; her body became rigid as her voice began to speak in a very gruff and manly fashion. She rose up, turned her head menacingly to one side, eyes glaring down at Greta.

"You are not welcome here. You do not deserve to be here. This is *my* domain. No one will ever move me from here. I will be here for eternity. Leave me! Leave this house now! I have been here for many hundreds of years. This is my home. It is mine! I will not let anyone take it. Ever! You will be forever cursed if you do!"

Greta was furious.

"If you think I am giving in to the likes of you, Barnabas Mowbrie, then you had better think again. We bought this property, fairly and squarely. It belongs to Max and to me. We want to live here in peace. Without the likes of you disturbing us and trying to drive us out! You shouldn't have murdered Willow. You should have led a peaceful, honest life. Not one of smuggling, deceit and murder! You're paying the price for your heinous crime. You are committed to a world of darkness, of evil. There is no escape for you. You made those decisions in your lifetime, you must adhere to them. Now, *you* leave Greenacres. *You* leave Willow and Evie alone. Let them be, they are the innocent victims. You are the perpetrator. You will pay for your sins. Leave this house now! Leave!"

As she spoke she flicked more holy water into the well. She turned and looked over at Rev Oli, who was unconscious. She grabbed the bible from his clasp and scanned to the pages from where he had been reading. She continued to recite the verses. Nonie was stood over the well. She had turned white and was holding on to her chest, the spirit of Barnabas had left her body.

"Keep going Greta! Keep speaking! Be steadfast! He is growing weaker, he is definitely growing weaker!" she gasped.

Greta continued her speech. Her eyes glanced first at Nonie and then at Rev Oli who was motionless. She reached for the cross and held it at arm's length.

"Be gone! In the name of the Father and the Son and the Holy Ghost! Be gone, forever!" she yelled and threw the remaining water into the well, along with the bottle as it fizzed and spat over the walls. The bottle reached the bottom of the well and smashed upon impact. Silence swept through the kitchen.

Greta's heart was pounding as she drew the cross close to her chest and held the bible in her other hand.

"Has he gone?" she whispered.

"I'm not sure. I think he might have," Nonie returned. "I can't pick up on him. The presence has gone. Oh nooo!"

Nonie resumed her rigid stance. Her eyes were large like saucers, lifeless, unblinking. Barnabas had taken over her body once more.

"I, Barnabas Mowbrie, smuggler, of Greenacres, will remain forever…"

Greta tried to converse with him.

"When did you die, Barnabas?" she tentatively asked. Nonie's body rose slightly off the ground as Barnabas communicated.

"A long time ago, many centuries ago. They found me; I was in the tunnel, guarding my goods."

"Was it another smuggler who killed you?" Greta continued.

"No, it wasn't another smuggler."

"Okay. So what did you store in the tunnel?"

"Brandy, tobacco, tubs of rum."

"Not any items of gold then?"

"No! It was too dangerous to deal in. I would have been caught, had it have been mine," Barnabas replied.

"Right. So who killed you? How did you die? Where did you die?" Greta went in for the kill.

"It was the holy man. He blocked off the tunnel, so I could not escape. I tried to dig my way out, but without success; it was difficult, I only have one hand. I died of starvation and thirst in that dark hellhole. He showed me no compassion. I cannot rest. I am damned to exist like this for eternity. It's all down to the holy man. He has placed this cursed anguish upon me and upon my soul."

"Are you trying to kill Rev Oli in revenge, then?"

Barnabas didn't answer.

"Barnabas, can you hear me?" Greta prompted.

"Yes, I hear you. Revenge is sweet!"

"But not for Willow; not for Evie."

"I did not kill this being you refer to as Evie!" Barnabas said angrily.

"Why did you kill Willow?"

"That interfering girl got in my way; she saw me hide it. I had to stop her!"

"Hide what? What did you hide?"

"The box," Barnabas murmured.

Greta shook her head in sadness. "But she was only a child, how could you be so callous, so cruel?"

"Life was also cruel to me," he replied.

"Who killed Evie, Barnabas? Did you see who killed Evie?"

Barnabas was silent. At length he spoke.

"It was he!"

Greta was puzzled. "Who?"

"The holy man!" As he answered, Nonie's left arm

raised up and her finger was pointing in the direction of Rev Oli.

"You can't be serious! Not Rev Oli, surely? You must be mistaken!" Greta was alarmed.

"It *was* him! He killed her!" Barnabas was insistent.

"You are scaring me now." Greta took a few steps away from the well.

"Be careful!" Barnabas warned.

Nonie slumped to the floor, her arm still outstretched in front of her.

"Nonie! Wake up! Come on, wake up!" Greta shook Nonie from her stony slumber.

"He's gone again, hasn't he?" Nonie mumbled. She raised her arm to her head. "Oh! My head really aches!"

"I'll get you an aspirin. We have a major problem," Greta added.

"Another one?" Nonie opened her eyes and focused on Greta.

"Barnabas was telling me, through you, that he saw Rev Oli murder Evie!"

"Oh that cannot be true, surely not? You can't believe everything he says." Nonie removed her glasses and rubbed her eyes. "Don't forget, he's full of evil. He's more than likely lying!"

"I don't know what to believe any more. What about this talk of the man with the same name?"

"Surname, yes, Mowbrie. But hang on a moment. Did Willow mean surname or first name do you think?"

"Well, that is a thought. I will try to raise her," Nonie stumbled to her feet. "I need to sit down first, though. I feel really terrible."

"Here," Greta dragged an old workbench belonging to the builders for her to sit on. It was covered in brick dust but Nonie was keen to sit, on no matter what. She plonked herself on to the bench and concentrated. At length, she spoke.

"Evie has just communicated with me. She is telling me that she too was murdered by a man with the same name. It wasn't Barnabas; it wasn't a holy man. She was strangled in the garden; left outside. The man who committed the crime was very clever, she tells me. Devious to disguise the fact that she died by strangulation. The perpetrator killed her in such a way that there was no trace of his hands pressing on her windpipe that calmly drew the life from her. The crime was never solved. Even the police remain baffled as to her death. It was recorded as death by misadventure by the coroner. The only mistake Evie made was being late paying her rent. She says she missed one monthly payment and her landlord, at the time, was furious with her. So upset that he… wait, what did you say, Evie?" Nonie stopped speaking and listened, her eyes closed. She nodded in acknowledgement. "Okay, okay, don't cry, Evie, please don't cry…" Nonie sighed.

"Who was the landlord?" Greta winced in anticipation.

Nonie opened her eyes.

"She is saying her landlord was Reverend Oliphant!"

"Yes, we know that. But I cannot believe Rev Oli would kill." Greta looked in horror towards where Rev Oli had been slumped on the floor.

"Is she sure? Are you sure, Nonie?"

Nonie nodded without answering.

Greta turned around just as Rev Oli had got to his feet and was staggering to the back door. The wound on his forehead oozed blood.

"Is this true, Rev Oli?" she yelled at him. "Did you kill Evie?"

"I am not listening to any more of this drivel! How can

you accuse me of committing a crime? I am a man of the cloth, for the Lord God's sake! I would not do such a terrible thing! Thou shalt not kill!" He continued to make his way to the door, bashing against the walls as he fled, he still clutched his chest. Blood trickled in rivulets down his face.

"Why would someone blame you, if there wasn't any truth in it?" Greta shouted.

"I have no idea, Gretel. Now I must leave this place!" Rev Oli reached for the handle of the door but Greta held it fast so he couldn't leave.

"No so fast, Reverend. I'm not convinced. We have three people stating you are Evie's murderer. Okay, so they are no longer of this world. And why would Nonie make up such a story? There's no need for her to lie."

"As I stated earlier, I have no idea. Now please, I must leave this place!" Rev Oli pushed Greta away from the door and staggered out into the garden.

"Why did you do it? Was it because Evie was late paying her rent? How could you?" Greta yelled.

"I didn't do it! *He* did it! He tried to blame me! I didn't do it!" shrieked Rev Oli. He turned around in the garden and pointed at the roof of Greenacres.

"You aren't making any sense. Who?" Greta was confused.

"Mowbrie! He was blackmailing me. He threatened me that I must get rid of my tenant, Evie. He constantly kept on and on at me to get her out of the cottage. He wanted the cottage for himself! I threatened me. I had to give him money; and lots of it!"

"To do what?"

Rev Oli was fanatical; he screamed. "It was him all along. He wanted rid of Miss Lukin, Evie! He wanted her out of the cottage so he could buy it from me for a pittance. He was so desperate to buy Greenacres. But I wouldn't let him have it. I just wouldn't!"

"This is crazy! How despicable!" Greta was shocked.

"Mowbrie drove me near to insanity! Constantly watching my every move, taunting me with threats! I was determined not to let him have Greenacres, at any cost!"

"Why didn't you tell the police?"

"I couldn't! He would have killed me; he pushed me into a corner. He told me if I said anything that he would kill me. He kept demanding more and more money from me. The only income I had was from the rent of Greenacres, and when Evie didn't pay, I feared for my life! Of what repercussions it might have on me. I couldn't bear to think of what he would do to me!"

"So he was blackmailing you. I can't believe all this can happen in such a quiet community."

"I am sorry, Gretel, to disappoint you. I... ahhhhh!"

Rev Oli dropped to the floor like a stone. He laid face down in the grass in the back garden. Greta rushed over and turned him gently on to his side. She felt for a pulse. She shook her head in disbelief.

"Oh no! Please no!" she hastily reached for her mobile phone and dialled 999.

"Police please, and an ambulance!"

After making the call, Greta held on to Rev Oli's hand. His pulse was very weak.

"Don't you die on me, Reverend. You can't escape that easily. There are a lot of unanswered questions you need to tell us. I know the police will be keen to speak with you."

Rev Oli eyes were closed. He was lifeless but he was still breathing, short and shallow breaths. The distant sound of emergency services sirens were becoming louder as they reached Greenacres. Two paramedics jumped out of an ambulance, ran over to where Rev Oli lay and took over.

"This is Reverend Oliphant. I think he's had a heart attack." Greta spoke in a whisper.

"Thank you, we'll treat him, now," the paramedic replied. A police car arrived on the scene shortly afterwards.

"Hello, I would like to report a crime, please, officer," Greta announced.

Chapter Twenty

Max had arrived earlier in the evening at Greta's parents' home. Nonie, Greta and Max were all sitting around the kitchen table. Each clutched a glass varying from a sherry schooner to a whisky tumbler. They sat in silence. Jeanne and Charles were in the drawing room. They too sat in silence. Greta's phone rang.

"Hello? Yes, this is Greta Berkley. Oh… no… oh, okay. Thank you for letting me know." She ended the call. Nonie looked at Greta.

"Was it the hospital?"

Greta nodded.

"How is he?"

"Rev Oli didn't responded to treatment; its not good news, I'm afraid. He died a few minutes ago. They couldn't revive him." She blinked away a tear. "This is terrible. He has left us in a complete quandary with so many unanswered questions. He held so much information, so many answers. This is just terrible!" Greta shook her head. Max held her hand.

"I'm sure he didn't intend to die, love. You can't blame him. From what you have told me he had a pretty bad time of things - both spiritually and in life. With Marcus

Mowbrie on his case all the time. His life must have been sheer hell."

"But why would Mowbrie treat him so badly? Why did he blackmail the Reverend?"

Max tried to make sense of the events.

"Because he obviously knows about the tunnel and what it harbours."

Nonie looked at Greta.

"Harbours? What do you mean?"

"The box in the room in the tunnel," Greta announced and took a sip from her glass.

"So you found something?" Nonie sat upright.

"Yes, we did and… uh?" Greta was stopped in her tracks from a swift kick from Max from under the table. "It was an old box, nothing in it. Disappointing."

Nonie wasn't convinced.

"There has to be much more to all this to make Marcus Mowbrie so desperate to buy the cottage."

"Hmm." Greta nodded.

"But you aren't going to tell me, are you? Even though Willow has already told me what you found!" Nonie retorted.

Greta glanced at Max. He returned her glance with a frown. He shook his head.

"Are you going to tell me? You don't have to, but, as I said, Willow has already told me. So you may as well spill the beans." Nonie persisted in a very convincing fashion.

"Okay," Greta conceded. "We found some gold in a box. We didn't move it out of the room in the tunnel. It's still down there. We thought it best to leave well alone, in case of any repercussions."

"Right, so *that* is Mowbrie's motive to get his hands on the cottage?" Nonie surmised.

"You knew that already, didn't you? You just told us!" Greta looked at Nonie in disbelief.

"Well, yes… I… Allegedly, from what information I managed to glean, Mr Mowbrie has a wife with a serious spending problem. She spends as much as she can. Much more than Mowbrie can earn. I think she is an addict."

"And?" Greta replied.

"It all makes sense now, he needed a house to keep her in her materialism." Nonie recalled her encounter with Mowbrie along the lane after her first visit to Greenacres. "It figures, that's why he didn't want me to investigate Greenacres."

"Rev Oli did say she was expensive to keep; that she had a problem… what do you mean, he didn't want you to investigate? When did you see Mowbrie?" Greta was startled by Nonie's words.

"He, Mr Mowbrie, stopped me in the lane, the first time I visited, when I drove over; he threatened me and told me not to find anything. He said he was concerned about what the locals would say; didn't want to upset a quiet community…"

"Rather he was concerned you would foil him and his involvement. What an evil man. A shallow bully!" Greta took a gulp of whisky and blinked as she swallowed.

Max was listening intently.

"What have you told the police, Greta?" He drained his glass.

"I told them we had been burgled, with the smashed window in the kitchen. I'm not so sure now. It might have been evil at work; or could it have been Mowbrie?" Greta looked at Max.

"So you didn't mention anything of past events at Greenacres then?"

"No. I didn't think it was relevant." Greta got up from the table and placed her glass on the work surface.

"Right. So we still have the problem of Barnabas on our hands, and Mowbrie." Max looked at Nonie.

"Is this Barnabas still at Greenacres?"

Nonie nodded.

"Yes, as far as I can tell. I have told Greta he is going to be very difficult to move on."

"Right. We need to get a plan together to oust this character from the cottage. I think it's time we get some sleep and tackle this in the morning." Max in turn got up from the table. He wandered into the drawing room where Jeanne and Charles were unusually quiet.

"Goodnight all. It's been a hectic day!" He smiled at Jeanne, who managed a weak smile.

Jeanne hesitated but spoke anyway, "Any news of the Reverend?"

Max nodded. "He didn't make it, Jeanne. Died about half an hour ago." He pursed his lips.

"Oh…" Jeanne held her hand to her heart. "God rest his soul."

"Damn shame, that. Goodnight, old boy," Charles replied. "Just off to bed myself," he added.

Chapter Twenty-One

"Are you any closer to believing there is an after life?" Greta was snuggled in bed with Max's arm draped loosely around her shoulders. She couldn't sleep.

"I'm finding it increasingly difficult not to believe, due to all the happenings at Greenacres. I still think, until I physically witness something, I will remain on the fence about the paranormal," Max replied.

"What do you think of Nonie?" she quizzed.

"Not so sure; she is a bit of a dark horse. I think there is much more to Nonie Spangler than meets the eye. We ought to tread very carefully; don't let her know too much. I think she could be quite dangerous."

"Really?" Greta turned and faced Max.

"Yes. There were certain things I picked up on when she was speaking this evening. Like when you mentioned the box and the gold."

"Sorry, I shouldn't have said anything about that." Greta was angry with herself with being so forthcoming with information.

"No, you shouldn't have. That's your gullibility showing its ugly head again. But it can't be helped now. We need to get to the bottom of this entire fiasco and get some normality back into our lives."

Greta nodded in silence.

"What are we going to do about the brick wall around the well; come to think of it, what about the window?"

Max thought for a moment.

"What's happening with the police?"

"I reported the broken window when they arrived. The officer said he would investigate and give me a call to take down some details and give me a crime reference number. They were also arranging for a glazier to board the window up, which I assume they have done. But I suppose we will find out in the morning. I expect they will ring with an update. It seems to be the least of our worries at the moment."

"That might be the case but we still have a criminal on the loose. Do they have any idea who might have broken it?" Max asked.

"No, not really. Unless, I am thinking it might have been our friendly farmer. It would be the sort of stunt he would try to pull, to try to frighten us. He must be pretty pissed off about the whole affair."

"Hmm, not so sure he would lower himself to do something like that. I wish I knew the reason why he was blackmailing Reverend Oli. It just doesn't make any sense." Max released his hold of Greta and turned over.

"I think his sole intention was to bully Reverend Oli into selling him Greenacres so he could get his hands on the gold. He must know everything about the place," Greta replied.

"Okay, well goodnight, darling. We'll talk more about all this in the morning. Oh, and try not to have any more dreams, please!"

Greta turned over and closed her eyes. It had been a harrowing experience for not only her but Nonie too. She snuggled into her pillow and soon after fell asleep.

□□□

"The same name, they shared the same name…" a voice in Greta's head repeated the words time and again.

"I know; but I still can't believe what you are telling me is true. He was such a gentle man; he couldn't possibly have murdered Evie; I need more proof."

"Perhaps the answers are already there…" the voice continued.

"Where?"

"All around you…"

"If you mean you have the answers, why don't you just tell me?"

"I have…"

"I don't understand."

"You must understand! You must! But… be careful!"

Greta woke up. She blinked a couple of times and reached across the bed. Max was silently sleeping. She sighed in relief.

"It was just a dream," she muttered to herself. "Thankfully, just a dream."

She jumped as a voice was calling her name.

"Greta! Greta? Are you awake?"

"Only just. What time is it?"

"Time to rise! Its 8 o'clock!" Jeanne boomed out from the bottom of the stairs.

"Thanks mummy!" Greta returned. Max stirred and opened his eyes.

"Early morning call, I take it?" He yawned and turned to cuddle Greta, who was trying to get out of bed.

"Big day; lots to do." She grabbed her dressing gown and headed for the bathroom.

Greta and Max were meeting with an army of fitters at Greenacres that morning. The carpet fitters were due to arrive at 9.30am to begin fitting the upstairs carpets and floor tiles in the ensuite bathrooms. The idea was to work from the top of the house to the ground floor, in between which time, the builders were expected to finish rebuilding the feature wall in the kitchen. Max hoped that if they all pulled together, this mammoth task might well be achieved without any further hitches. He was itching to get all the renovations finished at the cottage. He had the vision that Greta and he would be ready to move in by the end of the following week. Kindness aside, Max didn't want to overstay their welcome, staying with Greta's parents. They had been put upon enough in the ensuing past weeks. He wanted Greta to settle in to Greenacres and allay any fears or worries she might be experiencing.

They had a relaxing breakfast with Jeanne at the helm in the kitchen. They had to beg her not to provide another huge cooked breakfast and managed to curtail her to scrambled eggs on toast.

"When we move into Greenacres, we will get some chickens, mummy, so you can have fresh eggs for your cakes and breakfasts." Greta scraped the last morsel from her plate.

"Oh that would be wonderful, darling, won't it Maxim?" Jeanne beamed.

Max looked nonplussed. "Suppose so; but all they seem to do is eat, scratch everything to smithereens and crap everywhere!"

"Oh!" Jeanne looked deflated.

"Max!" Greta hissed. "Sorry mummy, he does have a romantic side… somewhere inside that head of his!"

"Not as far as bloody hens go!" Max mumbled and sipped his tea.

"And we could get some sheep, pigs… oh, perhaps I could have a horse!" Greta began to daydream.

Max raised an eyebrow.

"Right, I think we need to make tracks. Can you entertain Nonie for us, please, Jeanne? It will only be for the morning. It's time we left for Greenacres. Fitters will be arriving soon!" Max quickly changed the subject, finished his tea and got up from the table. "Thank you once again, Jeanne, for an outstanding breakfast." He walked over and pecked her on the cheek in gratitude.

"You're very welcome Maxim, as always. And I will try to keep Ms Spangler occupied. I will take her to the garden centre; perhaps show her some of the sights. She hasn't even stirred yet from her room. I have been upstairs to check."

"Thanks Jeanne, you're a star. We'll one day return the favour; I promise!" Max searchingly looked at Greta. She took this as a hint to get her coat.

"Thanks, mummy. I'll give you a call later on to let you know how things are going." Greta followed Max to the hallway.

"Bye!" they called out in unison.

Charles burbled his farewell from upstairs. He was midway through his ablutions.

"Bye dad!" Greta laughed.

"Is he still reading *The Times* up there?" laughed Max.

"Probably; knowing the father!" Greta replied and zipped up her coat.

Chapter Twenty-Two

As Max and Greta arrived at Greenacres, Greta's mobile phone rang. It was a withheld number.

"Mrs Berkley?"

"Yes, speaking," Greta replied.

"This is PC Henry. I have some news regarding the break-in at your property."

"Oh, I see. Would you please speak to my husband, Max, he's with me." Greta handed the phone to Max, placing her hand over the mouthpiece.

"It's the police," she warned him.

Max nodded and took the call. He continued to nod as he listened to the information being passed to him. He walked away from Greta and started to pace around the garden. He spoke in a lowered tone. At length Greta heard him say *goodbye*. He handed Greta her phone.

"So?" She was desperate to hear the news.

"Sorry, but you aren't going to like what I am about to tell you, love." Max sighed.

"Why? What do you mean? You are starting to worry me!" Greta felt a wrench in her stomach.

"The policeman told me they had received a report of a missing person."

"And? What has that got to do with us?"

Max swallowed and continued.

"They had an anonymous phone call in the early hours, reporting a man had gone missing from the local area. It was the same day as the break-in at Greenacres. When the glazier came, the police were still here. They could hear someone calling out. It was from all accounts very faint. They could hear the voice coming from the direction of the well…"

"Oh god!" Greta held her hands to her mouth. Her eyes were wide.

"They shone a torch down the well and saw a man's body lying on the ground. He had fallen down there. They called for an ambulance and got one of their people to climb down on a rope to reach him. When they did, they found he had broken his ankle. In a bit of a state from all accounts."

"Great! So now we have a bungling burglar. What the hell was he doing down there?"

"That's the thing. They cannot be one hundred per cent sure. You see the person they found was…" Max hesitated before he spoke again, "… was Leo…"

"What?" Greta was shocked. "Leo? How come?"

Max shook his head.

"Leo told them he was looking for you. You weren't in, so he decided to try one of the windows to get in but broke it by mistake. He said he called here when it was nearly dark. He didn't see the hole in the kitchen floor and fell through it."

Greta was shocked.

"So where is he now?" she whispered.

"In hospital; he's suffering from dehydration, obviously a broken ankle and hyperthermia. He's lucky to still be alive. He's been down there for days!" Max paced around the garden. "The police have telephoned your parents and they are at the hospital with him."

"Is Ardi with him too?" Greta asked, her mind flashed back to the incident with Rev Oli and Nonie. She remembered the voice from the well. She believed it to be Barnabas.

"I don't know," Max replied.

"Surely she would have realised that Leo wasn't around. Those two are joined at the hip most of the time." Greta was trying to fathom out Leo's story.

"Well, obviously not on this occasion."

"I wonder who made the anonymous call to the police." Greta was thinking aloud.

Max shrugged his shoulders and shook his head. "We need to get to the hospital to find out what exactly is going on. This is really, really weird."

"You go. I will have to stay here and wait for the fitters. We need to crack on with the work now. The sooner it is done, the sooner we can move in." Max squeezed Greta's hand. "Go on, I'll be fine."

"Are you sure?" Greta was concerned as Max was clearly deflated by the news.

"Quite. Go and see what your stupid brother was playing at." He tried to make a joke of the situation, which felt flat at Greta's expense.

"I will call you when I have more news." Greta ran to the car, jumped in and sped off up the track.

Max looked at his watch. It was nearly 9.30am. The fitters were due at any time. He continued to pace around in the garden. What had Leo been trying to do? The story he had spun to the police was pretty lame. Max wondered if it was one of Leo's attempted pranks that had gone horribly wrong. Or could it be more sinister than that? He suddenly thought about Nonie. If Greta's parents were at the hospital, where was Nonie?

"Hi Max!" a familiar voice called out from the driveway.

"Oh shit!" Max murmured and faked a smile. "Nonie! How did you get here?"

"Greta's parents had a phone call not long after you left and they had to leave immediately. They dropped me off on the way to go to the hospital. Have the police been in touch with you?" she gasped, trying to regain her breath. She held her hand tightly on her chest. "They phoned the house."

"Yes, they have, thank you for asking. As you are here, you may as well have a look around, see if you can see any-thing... if that's what you do. By the way, I am not totally convinced about all this," Max added, clearly wanting to vent his feelings on her presence.

"Not many people are, Max. But of course, I will do my very best," Nonie replied curtly.

"I'll leave you to have a ponder as the fitters have just arrived. Oh, by the way, keep everything low key, will you? I don't want any more gossiping about Greenacres."

Nonie smiled in acceptance and wandered slowly from room to room. She walked through the dining room to the drawing room. She stopped near the window and looked at the view. It was uninterrupted and she could quite clearly see in the distance the Smuggler's Hide Inn, high up on the hill. Periodically there was a flash of light as the window of a parking car caught the sunlight. It looked like a form of Morse code. She turned from the window and looked at the ornate mirror, which was leant against one of the walls. She bent down and picked it up and gazed at her reflection. She sighed and was about to replace it back on the floor when something caught her eye. She blinked and looked again. Clearly her own reflection was not alone. She nodded to herself and replied to the mirror.

"Is that you, Willow? If it is, you are very pretty."

The reflection of a young girl's face beamed back at Nonie. Her little white teeth shone like wild pearls. The girl giggled. Nonie smiled back at the little shade. Her smile quickly evaporated when the giggling became mocking laughter. The depth of the laugh was clearly not that of a child. Nonie stared again at the reflection; this time the child's face has transformed into the form of a male face. Rugged, unshaven and dirty. A toothy grin of blackened teeth and red raw gums snarled back at Nonie, black eyes and rugged weathered skin. Nonie was startled as the face began to speak. As it did so, Nonie noticed that, as the body materialised in front of her, the man only had one arm.

"You will not be rid of me, witch! Don't think you will ever get me to leave this place. You do not have the power or the strength. Leave this place!" it roared back at her.

Nonie stood her ground.

"Barnabas! You must be Barnabas," she murmured; taking heed of what Max had instructed. She tried not to raise any suspicions.

"Yes!" the reflection replied and in a split second, the mirror was snatched with invisible hands from Nonie's firm grasp. It was thrown up into the air, where it hit the ceiling and came crashing down on to the uncarpeted floor. It smashed into hundreds of shards, which spread like a huge cobweb all over the floor.

"Oh! Ha, ha! You ought to be more careful!" Barnabas mocked. His voice was travelling around and around the room until Nonie was immersed by his uncontrollable laughter. "Seven years' bad luck; but not as many years of bad luck that I have suffered! Don't try to cross me, heathen!"

Nonie turned around and around in the room like she was being spun in a vicious, endless spiral. She held her head as the feeling of vertigo made her plunge to the floor. She landed on a shard of glass, which bit into her forearm. She winced from the pain and tried to remove the offending glass. She held her breath as she carefully removed the glass and threw it onto the floor. As she reached for a tissue to mop the speck of blood on her arm, she felt another sharp pain on the side of her face; and another, and another, until the side of her face, arm and legs had been pierced by numerous flying shards of glass; each in turn had lifted from the floor in succession and had been expertly aimed at Nonie like spear-shaped javelins. Nonie screamed and ran from the drawing room. She found Max in the kitchen talking to one of the fitters. Max took one look at her and immediately urged her outside to the garden.

"What the hell is going on?" he hissed. "Didn't you listen to what I said earlier? I don't want any fuss from you!" He stopped as he looked at Nonie's blood-stained face. She dropped to the floor in pain. "What the hell has happened to you?" Max was horrified by Nonie's injuries.

"I'm so sorry, Max. I tried not to make a scene. It was the mirror in the drawing room. It fell to the floor. I think I must have fainted and fell on to the glass," Nonie lied. She panted with the pain as each shard clung to her flesh.

"You need to get to the hospital. I will call for an ambulance. I can't leave here." Max fumbled for his mobile phone and dialled 999.

"Max, please don't worry. I'll be fine. It is just a few scratches from the glass. Nothing I can't deal with. Besides… I also can't leave here…"

Max hesitated before he pressed the call button.

"Why can't *you* leave here?" he asked incredulously.

"Because of… well, because of Barnabas. Sorry, but it was him who caused the mirror to shatter. It is his way of trying to get rid of me."

"I don't believe this!" Max held his hands to his head, still clutching his phone.

"You must trust me on this, Max," Nonie panted.

"Seems like I don't have any choice. But I am telling you, God help you if this is one of your stunts!" Max cancelled the call and placed his phone back into his trouser pocket. "Here, go to the bathroom. Take this and keep your mouth shut!" He handed Nonie a pack of tissues. "There is a first aid box in the kitchen, I will bring it up to you. Go and get yourself cleaned up," he ordered.

Nonie obeyed and began to walk upstairs. Max shook his head in disbelief. He was beginning to regret the day Greta had set eyes on Nonie. He returned to the kitchen where the fitters had begun.

"Are you clear on what to do, guys? If you make a start in the top bedrooms and stairs, ensuite and then the bedrooms on the first floor," Max instructed.

"Yes thanks, boss. No problem. Uh, is everything all right with that lady? She looked a bit shaken up."

"Oh her, yes. Bit of a liability, that one. Broke a mirror, got a few cuts from the glass. I am going to sort her out now. I don't know; some people!" he joshed and hoped he had allayed any suspicion from the fitters. Instead they laughed and took their tools upstairs to start laying the carpets. They talked amongst themselves. Max sighed with relief. He thought about Greta and what was happening with Leo.

□□□

"Are you going to tell me honestly what the bloody hell you were playing at?" Greta yelled at her brother, who was lying in a hospital bed with his ankle suspended.

"Oh. Hello sis," Leo weakly replied.

"Don't *hello sis* me, you little idiot!" Greta slammed her handbag on to the bed and dragged a chair up so she could sit as close to Leo's face as she could.

"Darling, your brother is very poorly!" Jeanne scolded as Greta pushed her mother to one side.

"My arse he's poorly. You will do anything to gain attention, eh, Leo? I'm right, aren't I?" Greta snarled. Her face was inches away from Leo's as she pretended to kiss his cheek.

"Please, Greta, be a little more compassionate. He had a terrible fall, a dreadful shock!" Jeanne tried to reason.

"Oh and I wonder why he had such a terrible fall? Maybe it was because he was trying to *break into our home*! So, what were you trying to achieve, little brother? Do tell, the suspense is surprisingly, like myself, wanting to kill you!"

Leo smiled awkwardly.

"It was nothing more than what I told you earlier. I arrived at the cottage, you weren't there, so I tried to get in by opening the kitchen window." Leo took a deep breath. "But it wouldn't budge and somehow, I put my elbow through it, broke the glass…"

"You must be super-strong, then. The window was double glazed!" Greta yelled.

"Darling! Please! Think of the other patients!" Jeanne tried to speak.

"Not now, mummy… please!" Greta tried to stay calm.

"Well, it broke quite easily. Then when I climbed through, it was pitch black. I didn't notice the hole in the floor and went headlong through it. Felt like I was pushed. Next thing I know, I am at the bottom of a pit."

"Isn't that a shame?" Greta mocked. "Poor little Leo! My heart bleeds for you! Well, it serves you right for breaking in. You have your just reward. Hopeless! Talking of hopeless, where is Hardy?"

Leo didn't answer. Jeanne answered for him.

"She had to go back home, darling. She is out of the country."

Greta thought for a while.

"Have you phoned her to let her know what my stupid brother has done?"

"Yes, I left a message on her phone. But I haven't had a reply back. Apparently the signal is pretty terrible in Poland."

"I'm sure she will be beside herself when she hears the news!" Greta's sarcasm was too much for Charles, who was sitting quietly at the other side of Leo's bed.

"Enough now, Greta. I think you have said enough," he quietly but firmly concluded. "Leo is tired, he needs some sleep."

Leo acknowledged his father with a degree of relief on his face and Greta took the hint to leave. As she reached the door, she turned and pointed her finger at Leo.

"I will get the truth out of you, no matter what it takes!" she warned and slammed the door behind her. "Heaven help you when I find out!"

Jeanne sighed and plumped Leo's pillow for the umpteenth time. She reached across and offered him a drink from a plastic beaker. Leo obliged, closed his eyes and sipped the water.

"We'll come back and see you tomorrow, darling." She kissed the top of Leo's head. "Get some rest now. It will do you good," she soothed.

"Bye ma, bye dad," Leo whispered and closed his eyes. As soon as his parents had left the room, Leo opened his eyes and blinked. He reached over to the bedside locker and took out his mobile phone. He checked it for messages. There was one from Ardi.

Have they gone yet? it read.

Leo replied with, *yep*.

I am coming in, beeped the response.

Leo swallowed and held his breath.

Chapter Twenty-Three

"You have really, really messed up!" Ardi was stood over Leo's hospital bed. "A seemple task, Mr Mowbrie instructed you to do and you mess it up! Thees is not good, Leo, not good at all!" she snapped.

"How was I to know how deep the bloody hole was?" Leo tried to reason.

Ardi grabbed the suspended stirrup that held Leo's plastered ankle and wrenched it hard so he was dangling from the bed in pain. She leant over until her head was level with his.

"You're so stupeed, Leo. I thought you could be trusted with this seemple task. Clearly not! This puts a much different light on things now!" Ardi swiftly let go of the winch and Leo flopped back on to the bed. He landed on his side.

"What do you mean?" he whispered, trying to correct his position.

"It means, my dearest, that we are in beeg trouble!" Ardi hissed. Her petite features were screwed up into a darkened frown.

"We are?" Leo responded and held on to his leg for support. He tried to gain his composure but his ankle was throbbing.

"I need to act very fast. Beefore it is way too late!"

Ardi paced around the ward, her hands folded behind her back.

"When you were in the passage, did you see anything?" she demanded.

Leo shook his head. "No, it was too dark. I was in so much pain. It was as much as I could do to survive in that hellhole. Lucky I had a packet of sweets and my fags to keep me going."

"And has your sister bought your excuse?" Ardi peered sharply at him.

"I'm not sure. She is pretty pissed with me about the whole situation. But I think I have convinced both her and the olds that you have gone back to Poland. So you are completely out of the picture." Leo tried to humour Ardi, who was still deep in thought.

"Hmm. So it will all be down to me to sort thees mess out!" she concluded.

Leo nervously cackled.

"You're not serious?"

Ardi stood upright and looked indignant. She placed her hands on her hips and flicked the collar of her black leather jacket so it stood to attention.

"Why not? You made a beeg mess of things. It's up to me now, right?"

"But how are you going to do it? What if the same thing happens to you?"

Ardi smiled knowingly as she spoke. "Because it won't 'appen to me. I am skilled, I have the courage." She tapped her finger against her forehead.

"Have you a plan?" Leo dared to ask.

"Of course!" Ardi snapped. "Do you think I am that stupeed?"

"No, no, I don't." Leo bit his lip.

"I will go there tonight. When they have all gone. I will get the box."

"In heaven's name, be careful, then. I can't help you if things go wrong," Leo tried to reason. "What happens if it's not there?"

"Don't woray. I weel be just fine, course it weel be there; I am confident," Ardi announced. "I will call you when I have result," she added and planted a kiss on Leo's cheek. "Get well soon, my dearest!" she whispered in his ear and took a harsh, swift bite of his lobe flesh. "Weesh me luck!"

"Uh, good luck," Leo mumbled. He held on to his ear and rubbed it. A small speck of blood stained his pillow.

Ardi strode across the hospital car park and mounted a waiting black motorbike. She tapped the driver on the helmet and they sped out on to the open road.

□□□

Greta and her parents arrived at Greenacres in their respective cars. They walked across the driveway.

"Mummy, I know that for a fact Leo is lying." Greta's voice was raised as she spoke. "I know him inside out. He's not telling us the truth! I could tell by his expression. You don't realise how devious he is."

"Well, it seems feasible that he would do a stupid prank to try to frighten you. Probably spider related. As it is still fresh in his mind, you know, the wedding…"

"Yes!" Greta interrupted. "You don't need to remind me, mummy." She shook her head in frustration.

"He has a girlfriend. They rent a nice flat together. He has a good job. Do you think he is jealous of Max and me?"

"I don't know, darling. I can't think of any reason for him to be jealous. As you know, the father and I have always treated you both equally."

"I know; but does he really appreciate that fact? There's absolutely nothing to stop him buying his own place with Ardi. He probably doesn't want to commit to anything, knowing him. He's always been a bit of a free spirit, hasn't he?"

"Run the poor boy some slack, old girl," Charles muttered. "He's had an accident. It has probably shaken him up enough already."

"Yes, okay, daddy," Greta rolled her eyes. "But there is something odd about the whole affair and I can't place my finger on it. Anyway, let's see how things are shaping up here."

She led the way into the kitchen.

"Max! Max? Are you here?" Greta called. She could hear the occasional tapping noise made from a mallet coming from upstairs.

"Hi, yes, will be down in a tick," Max's voice returned. He joined Greta and her parents in the dining room.

"Hi darling, Jeanne, Charles. Well, things are going very well. The fitters have laid the carpets in the top rooms. They are just finishing off the ensuite bathroom's tiled floor. It's really beginning to take shape now. They are off in a moment, so you can inspect their handiwork!" He kissed Greta on the cheek. "How's Leo?"

"Hmmph! Still alive!" Greta sulkily replied.

"Greta!" Jeanne was shocked and decided to carry on the conversation. "He is comfortable, thank you, Maxim, for asking. I think he will be in hospital for a few days. It was a particularly nasty break."

"Luckily!" Greta mumbled.

Charles glared at her. Greta decided not to continue her verbal attack.

"Did he say what he was doing at Greenacres?" Max was interested in the excuse.

"Only that he was trying to find Greta, but when she wasn't in he accidentally broke the window, to get in. Thought he could open it without damaging it. Then he got in, fell down the well hole or rather he says he was pushed and, well the rest is history."

"Right…" Max looked at Greta's disbelieving mouthing of *no he didn't* and her hand, slanted sideways, making a cutting sign beneath her neck. He looked towards the stairs. "Ah, the fitters are coming downstairs. Come on, have a look at what they've done. It's superb! I'll see you guys in the morning!"

"Right, boss. We will finish the next floor tomorrow, nice easy job!" the fitters waved their goodbyes.

Max led Jeanne and Charles upstairs. Greta followed.

"Max," Greta called after him. "Where is Nonie?"

Max thought before he spoke.

"Umm, she arrived here earlier. She had a bit of an accident."

"What sort of accident?" Greta was concerned. Nonie's track record of accidents wasn't good.

"She broke a mirror," Max replied through Jeanne and Charles as they climbed the stairs.

"Where?"

"In the drawing room."

"Oh no," Greta wailed. "Is she all right? Where is she now?"

"Here, Greta," Nonie appeared, ashen-faced, from behind the bathroom door.

"Oh Nonie! What happened? You look terrible!" Greta held on to Nonie's small frame. "What happened to your face? You have cuts all down the side of it!" She inspected Nonie's wounds.

"I'll be fine. It's superficial," she bravely announced and managed a smile.

189

"You ought to go to hospital; really you should."

"No! I'm fine, seriously. I can't leave."

"This way!" Max ushered Jeanne and Charles to the second floor of bedrooms. "Greta!"

"I'll be up in a moment," she replied, still holding on to Nonie's shoulders. "Tell me what happened, now!" Greta insisted.

"It was Barnabas. I saw the mirror in the drawing room. I took hold of it and I thought it was Willow's reflection I could see, then it morphed into a man's face, pure evil. All of a sudden, the mirror was taken from me. It must have been him. He threw it up into the air and it smashed on the floor, then bits of glass were flying around everywhere. I got hit by a few pieces, on my face, my arms." She pointed at her other wounds. "Max helped me get the shards out. I think most of them are gone now. But it was really frightening. He is definitely still here, Greta. I don't know what else I can do."

"You must help us!" Greta shook Nonie as she spoke. "We have to get him out of this place. He can't remain here. It will be terrible."

"I know, but I am running out of energy with him. He is so powerful."

"What about a séance?" Greta suggested.

Nonie looked at Greta in surprise.

"Absolutely no way! Don't even think about carrying out a séance. You would most certainly be inviting trouble, not only from Barnabas but also from other spirits. Open one of those ouija boards and heaven help you. No, don't let it cross your mind Greta. It would be very bad news."

Greta made a face and held up her hands.

"Okay, point made. It was only a suggestion."

"You mentioned something about a box in the tunnel," Nonie began.

Greta was cautious. "Yes."

"Was it really empty?" Nonie asked.

Greta paused. "No."

"What was in it?"

"Just old stuff." Greta was uncomfortable by Nonie's questioning.

"What sort of old stuff?" she continued.

"I don't know, I couldn't really see. It was too dark there to work out what it was," Greta bluffed and prayed for Max to save her from certain doom.

"Willow told me it was filled with gold," Nonie smirked.

"Did she?" Greta felt her face redden.

"Lots of gold."

"Right."

"She was right, wasn't she, Greta?"

"Ah! There you are! How are you feeling, Nonie? You are looking better than you did. Have you put some anti-septic cream on those wounds?" Max breezed down the stairs. Greta heaved an inward sigh of relief. She turned away and faced the wall, her hand to her head. She swallowed and regained her composure.

"Yes, Nonie is doing well, aren't you?" Greta walked towards Max and linked arms with him. She smiled triumphantly at him.

"I think we've all had enough for one day, don't you? Come on, let's get back to your parents' house. Jeanne has invited us all for supper. Isn't that nice?"

"One of my specialities, chicken curry and basmati rice!" Jeanne chirped as she helped Charles down the flight of winding stairs from the second floor. "The carpets are divine, darling! Go and see for yourself!" Jeanne urged Greta towards the stairs. "We'll take Nonie back to the house in our car!"

"Thanks mummy. We'll follow on shortly!" Greta called

out. In a hushed whisper she stared at Max. "You saved me from certain trouble!"

Max frowned and took hold of her shoulders.

"What do you mean? Your mother's curries aren't that bad, are they?"

Greta shook her head.

"No, silly. Nonie was starting to pry about the…" she lowered her voice even more. "… You know, the treasure," she spoke out of the side of her mouth.

"She is like a terrier with a bone, isn't she; she just won't let go!" Max was annoyed. "This business with the mirror. She says it was because of this Barnabas thing. I think she has a screw loose. She clearly dropped the thing and fell onto some glass and cut herself."

"She is convinced she can't leave here until Barnabas leaves Greenacres," Greta said.

"I think it's a load of twaddle. Sorry, darling, but I still think she is a fake! Any way, what do you think of this?" Max opened the door to the top bedroom and Greta walked in with her mouth gaping. "Slip your shoes off!" Max warned.

"Oh, it is beautiful! It's really beautiful. What a difference! The carpet goes so well with the décor. I love it, I really adore it!"

Greta walked into the bedroom. Her feet almost disappeared into the softness and depth of the biscuit-coloured pile. It had been beautifully fitted and the smell of newness filled the air.

"They have even vacuumed the fluff off the surface," Greta waltzed around the room and held her arms out straight in front of her. "I am impressed with how professional and sumptuous this is!" she cooed.

"I thought you'd like it, only the best for you, my sweet." Max took hold of her hands and drew her towards him.

He tenderly kissed her on the lips. "You know we have to christen every room when it's finished, don't you?"

Greta smiled and held Max close to her.

"Of course and I can't wait!"

Their noses touched as they gazed into each other's eyes.

"Happy?" Max gently asked.

"You bet!" was the reply.

"Come on, have a look at the tiles in the ensuite. They look great too." She walked into the room and gasped in horror.

Max pushed Greta to one side. He stopped in the doorway.

"Shit! What the hell has happened here?" he exclaimed.

The newly tiled walls and floor were completely daubed in large, red spidery writing. Greta shuddered and held on to Max for all she was worth. Max was shocked as he read out what was spelt in front of him.

"Be careful."

Greta closed her eyes and opened them again in hope she was dreaming. Max leant against the door. He held his hand to his head.

"But I don't understand. How could this have happened? *When* could this have been done? We've been here all the time. Your parents didn't say anything about it…"

"Oh Max, this is horrible. Who is doing this to us? Why are they doing this?"

"I don't know, darling. But I don't like what I see." Max stared at the wall. He turned to Greta. "Not a word to your parents. We don't want to worry them any more. This is starting to get very serious!" He thought for a moment then decided not to say anything.

Chapter Twenty-Four

Leo was asleep when his mobile phone vibrated from underneath his pillow. It was a text from Ardi. He focussed on the message. It read, *are you awake?* He tapped the screen on his phone to reply.

I am now.

The phone vibrated a few seconds later. *I'm at the cottage*

Leo responded. *Take care!*

Bleep.

xxx

Leo placed his phone back under his pillow and closed his eyes. He tried not to visualise what Ardi's plan was and how she would execute it.

"What did you say to him?" a familiar voice gently asked Ardi. Ardi turned over in the bed and held on to the masculine frame that was lying beside her.

"I told him I was at the cottage," she replied, and draped her leg over his body.

"There's a good girl. It's all going to plan."

Ardi sighed.

"Yees, Marcus. Eet is all going to plan!"

Marcus Mowbrie swiftly turned Ardi on to her back and kissed her firmly on the mouth.

"That is bloody fantastic news. Now, where were we?"

They continued to kiss until Ardi pushed Marcus away from her.

"Enough! It is time! I need to go!" she announced and rose from the bed. She quickly dressed as Mowbrie watched her.

"Shame. I was just enjoying our little... liaison," he replied.

"I know. But you can 'ave more of me lateer." She zipped her leather jacket up to her neck. "Thees task is not complete."

"I like your sense of determination," he smiled.

"And I like the thought of staying in thees country," was the response.

"Ring me," Mowbrie insisted.

"If I can, I weel." Ardi bent over the bed and hovered above Mowbrie's face. Her nose was above his forehead. He lunged towards her. Ardi swiftly moved away and wagged her finger at him.

"Uha." she shook her head. "Later."

Mowbrie looked like a spoilt schoolboy and pouted in disappointment.

"You give me money; enough for a house; I get you the gold!" She flounced out of the bedroom and closed the door behind her.

"You are such a tease! Good luck!" he called after her. But there was no response.

Ardi's motorcycle rider was patiently waiting for her outside. She ran towards him and with a thumb held in the air, he started the engine and they rode off in the darkness.

□□□

"Do you think the writing will be easy to clean off the walls?" Greta asked Max. They were sitting in the car in the driveway of Greta's parents' house.

"Yes, I'm sure it will. Look, don't let this upset you. I will get to the bottom of this. I am damn sure no-one is going to stop us living at Greenacres, be they alive or dead. Someone's head will roll for this."

"I hoped you'd say that." Greta squeezed Max's thigh. "What's the plan?"

Max thought for a moment. "We need to get Nonie over to Greenacres tomorrow. Get her to raise this Barnabas character to try and strike up a deal with him. All this has got to be over the gold. It's the only thing I can think of that is keeping him there. If we tell her say to him we'll leave it where it is, then maybe he will leave us alone. We can then fill in the passage, cap the top of the well and put an end to it. What do you think?"

"I think that's the best option. Perhaps, as you say, he might then leave us alone. What about Willow and Evie?"

"I shouldn't worry about them; they aren't sinister spirits, are they? I think I could live with a couple of female ghosts in the cottage."

"Sounds kinky!" Greta felt a little easier after their discussion.

"Hmm." Max was thoughtful. Greta slapped his arm.

"Don't even go there!" she warned. "Come on, I can smell the curry from here!"

"Jeez, I bet it's potent as you like!" Max laughed.

"Course it will be! It is mummy's speciality! An age old recipe handed down from the Raj!"

Chapter Twenty-Five

Greta shook Max awake.

"Come on. Time to get up."

"Hmm? Oh, hi darling, I was just having this fantastic dream about two female ghosts… but I can't tell you what they were doing to me!" Max turned over with a smile on his face.

"Yeah right, that is definitely in your dreams!" Greta replied and placed a cup of tea on the bedside cabinet.

"No, seriously, it was, well… quite real."

"Really?" Greta stood in the doorway with a puzzled expression on her face.

"No, silly, I'm joking!" Max waited for the expected response.

"Breakfast is ready." Greta chose to ignore Max and returned downstairs.

After showering, Max joined the breakfast table with acknowledgements from all who were sat around it. Greta stared at Max in an odd fashion. Her face was thunderous. She got up from the table and walked around to where Max was sitting.

"What is that?" She pointed at him.

"What?" Max looked surprised.

"*That!*" Greta pointed to a large mark on his neck. She made an indentation in his skin with her finger, causing the blemish to temporarily pale.

"I can't see from here," he proffered.

"Well I can see it from *here!*" Greta stomped back to her chair.

"Everything all right, darling?" Jeanne looked up from the daily newspaper she was skimming through.

"Yes," snapped Greta and noisily clanked her cereal spoon against her teeth. As she did so, she realised what she had done and the response she would endure.

"Greta!" Jeanne howled in despair. "Please! Not like the father!"

"Sorry mummy. A situation caused it." Greta glared at Max, who sat looking baffled at his angry wife.

The breakfast was eaten in silence. Nonie broke the silence.

"Are we still on for today?" She cautiously looked around the table.

"Yes," Max replied. "D day. I need to be over at Greenacres to let the fitters in again this morning. They're going to get the first floor bedrooms completed today so if you can be over to the cottage this afternoon, we can get the job done."

"Sounds intriguing, Maxim." Jeanne smiled.

"Yes, it probably will be, Jeanne. But hopefully with positive results."

"Good luck." Jeanne began to collect the crockery from the table, shifting Charles and his newspaper to one side as she busied herself with the washing up.

Greta was still sulking over what appeared to be a love bite on Max's neck.

"Would you be able to take me over to Greenacres,

Greta?" Nonie asked. "And I need to go back home today. I have some longstanding appointments coming up over the next few days."

"Hurrah! Thank god for that!" Charles mumbled from behind his newspaper.

Jeanne looked embarrassed and cluttered the crockery in an attempt to stifle Charles and his outburst. She made a point of coughing and clearing her throat.

"Oh dear, must have a tickle!" she chattered and dug her elbow into Charles's ribs as she walked past him.

"Ergh!" Charles croaked and looked at Jeanne in distaste. He flicked the pages of his paper and continued to read.

"Yes, that's absolutely fine, Nonie. I'll collect you when the fitters are finished." She chose to ignore her parents.

Greta was relieved that at last Nonie was going home. She had been staying with the family for the past few days and Greta could see her parents, particularly Charles, were beginning to tire of her presence. Max's patience was also waning. Greta prayed that Nonie could finally rid them of Barnabas from the cottage. "I will go upstairs and pack my belongings," Nonie rose from the table. "Thank you, Jeanne, for another lovely breakfast. I will truly miss them when I go home. You have made me so welcome in your lovely home."

Jeanne smiled with gritted teeth as she could see Charles was about to make another of his comments.

Greta and Max were outside getting ready to leave for Greenacres. Max was packing a few tools in the boot of the car.

"If we go over to meet the fitters this morning, then you can come back and collect Nonie. Make sure she is ready to leave here on time."

"She will be. She is packing her bag as we speak," Greta replied.

"Hand me that bucket of stuff, will you?" Max spoke without turning around.

"Just think, we will soon be living at Greenacres," Greta thought aloud.

"Yep. It will only be a matter of a few more days of staying with your parents."

"It will be blissful!" Greta dreamed.

"Especially if it is spook-free!" Max closed the boot of the car. "Okay, let's make tracks."

They drove from the house to Greenacres. It was an overcast day with a cloud-filled sky. The Island looked particularly remote as the mainland was hidden in the grey and gloom of sea mist. A lone foghorn blared in the distance in the Solent. As they reached the driveway, they could see the fitters had already arrived and were unpacking their vans.

"Good morning guys. I'll just open up for you," Max called across the yard as he drove in and parked the car.

"Morning, boss; Mrs Berkley," the fitters chimed in unison.

"Happy chaps, aren't they?" Greta found it a refreshing change to see amiable workmen that didn't grunt and groan all the time. She found the chore of tea making not so laborious as it was when the builders were working at Greenacres.

"So far," Max cautiously replied.

He walked across the garden and opened the back door to the kitchen.

"Let's hope we don't have any more… surprises… oh shit!"

"What?" Greta ran over to where Max was stood.

"Look!" Max pointed to the floor. "We have a flood!"

"I don't believe it!" Greta shook her head in despair.

Max rolled up his trouser legs, took off his shoes and sloshed through a puddle of water. He looked around in the kitchen. Nothing was immediately obvious until he noticed the sink and the cascading water. He felt a sense of relief, as it was nothing more than an accident. The cold tap was running steadily. He turned it off and pulled the plug from the sink. The water dispersed rapidly.

"It's not the end of the world, darling, just a tap running. It hasn't been like it for long. The floor should soon dry out. We must have left it on last night." He sounded upbeat.

"And I was ready for another onslaught from the unknown." Greta breathed a sigh of relief.

The fitters filtered in and began to lay the carpets in the main bedrooms. Max and Greta climbed the second winding staircase, armed with cleaning products to clean the walls of the ensuite bathroom from the vandalised scrawl. They reached the door to find the light was switched on inside the room.

"I thought I'd turned the light off yesterday." Max tried to think back to his actions.

"It is easy to forget. Being a windowless room and the anxiety we were put through yesterday," Greta reassured him and walked into the room. She gave a gasp.

"Bloody hell!"

"What?" Max joined her.

Together they stared at the walls.

"Has someone been in here?" Greta whispered.

"I don't know, but that is really odd." Max walked over to the walls and touched them.

There were no signs of the red writing on any of the walls in the room. All the walls were clean and sparkling.

"I'm not complaining." Max rubbed his chin. "But how could this happen? Do you think we have a guardian cleaning ghost to add to our collection?"

"It's one of life's little mysteries," Greta smiled. "Never to be solved."

"Well at least they have saved us some time, we can be getting on with other things."

"Like moving a few bits and pieces in," Greta suggested.

"Yes, why not. There are some things in the car if you want to start bringing them in."

"Ooh, this is fabulous news!" Greta enthused. "It seems like we are starting to move in!"

"That's the plan," Max picked up the cleaning goods and headed for the stairs. "I think we will concentrate on clearing up that water in the kitchen and back porch and I will have a look at the wall around the well, too."

Throughout the day the fitters carried on stalwartly with their job of carpet fitting, making a tremendous job. The transformation again was immense and Greenacres began to resemble a family home. Greta and Max mopped the water from the kitchen and concentrated on hanging curtain rails, curtains and tiebacks in the upper rooms. A wooden blind was easily installed in the bathroom. The fitters completed their work just after lunchtime. Greta and Max were delighted.

"Thank you so much, guys; you have done a cracking job. We will certainly recommend you to our family and friends," Max announced as he shook hands.

"Lovely place this is, boss. We hope you will enjoy living here. Bet you will!"

They drove off in their respective vans and disappeared up the track in a trail of dust.

"It's getting close to half past three. Time you were thinking about collecting Nonie," Max reminded Greta, who was wandering around the cottage, clutching her sides and staring at the new carpets.

"It makes it so cosy, doesn't it?" she replied in a trance.

"Yes, it's really great." Max smiled as he watched Greta gliding around in her bare feet on the carpets.

"Even the drawing room is so much more homely. Particularly now that horrible mirror isn't in there any more."

"Yes, the remains are in the dustbin. So it won't frighten you again. Hey, maybe you caught sight of your own reflection and that's what scared you. It might have even scared Nonie! Seeing your ugly mug staring out at her!"

Greta picked up one of her shoes and threw it at Max. Her aim was poor and it missed him by miles.

"Mind the floor. Don't want any dust on it!" he laughed.

"I don't deserve you!" Greta replied.

"No, you don't. After all, who in their right mind would have bought you a country cottage in the middle of nowhere on a beautiful island?"

"I really do appreciate everything, Max. I might not show it at times, but believe me, I do."

Max walked over and took Greta into his arms. He gazed into her eyes, held her face between his hands and gently kissed her.

"I would do anything for you, you daft creature. You might be a complete pain in the arse; but I wouldn't have you any other way!"

"You'll have me in tears next," Greta whispered.

"No, I couldn't cope with any more water. We've had enough in the kitchen to sink a small ship. Now, go and collect Nonie. We have one more job to do and you know exactly what it is."

"Okay. I won't be long."

Max kissed Greta on the cheek.

"Missing you already!"

She raised her hand as she walked out of the back door.

"Shoes!" Max reminded her.

"Thanks, nearly forgot!" Greta hopped on one foot and then the other, replacing her shoes on her feet, after retrieving her failed missile from the corner of the porch.

"Keys!" Max yelled.

"In the car," was the response.

"Bye!"

Chapter Twenty-Six

Nonie, Max and Greta were stood in the kitchen around the well. Nonie was looking around the room. Max stared at the hole in the floor and Greta was wringing her hands in anticipation.

"Okay, what's the plan, Nonie?" Max broke the silence.

Nonie looked incredulously at Max. "Plan? You can't plan anything with the spirit world. It just happens. He will make things happen. We'll just have to be patient."

"I thought all good investigators had a plan! Ah well, so how long will it take?" Max pursed his lips.

"Who knows… hang on a minute…" Nonie took a deep breath and closed her eyes. "I think we might have something."

She paused and remained still. The kitchen was in silence. At length, Nonie nodded as though she was being given an instruction.

"I have just been in communication with Willow and Evie."

"And?" Max prompted.

"They are saying Barnabas is here, but I can't pick up on him yet."

"Perhaps he is playing hide and seek!" Max was inflicted with a thump on the arm from Greta.

"Now is not the time to mess about, Max!" Nonie sternly warned. "Not if you want Barnabas out of here."

Max put up his arms in submission.

"Okay, okay, I will shut up."

Nonie closed her eyes again and began to concentrate.

"Shall I put the kettle on?" Max asked.

"Shush! Please, Max!" Nonie opened her eyes and glared at him. She resumed her stance and closed her eyes once again.

"Are you sensing anything, Greta?" she whispered.

Greta looked at Max.

"Sorry, no. Nothing."

"Okay…" Nonie replied. "Are you sure?"

"Yes! I am completely sure."

There was a faint rumbling sound.

"Sorry! That's my stomach!" Max burst out laughing.

"Oh, for the love of god!" Nonie opened her eyes. "I really cannot concentrate on anything with you here, Max. Can you step outside for a while, please? I need to clear my head."

"Sure. In fact, I'll nip up to the pub and grab some sandwiches. I'm starving. Do you want me to bring you anything back?" He looked at Greta, who was shaking her head in annoyance.

"See you later, Max." She indicated for him to leave by looking at the door, before Nonie lost her temper.

Nonie waited until Max was driving up the track before she spoke.

"Sorry, Greta. Max was blocking everything. He has a lot of negative energy around him and it doesn't help when I am trying to summon Barnabas."

"It's all right, Nonie. Max is not the best person to have around at a time like this. He thinks it's all a big joke. Anyway, how are you going to move Barnabas on?"

"I think a lot of the trouble is centring around the box of bits in the tunnel. He appears to be protecting them. I think if we were to move them from the cottage, he might just leave too."

"Well, we'll have to wait until Max comes back as the box is quite heavy and I haven't the strength to carry it up the ladder from the tunnel. I can't see that it would make much difference. He did say before that he only stored rum and tobacco there, nothing more than that." Greta didn't want to entertain Nonie being involved in the knowledge of the gold.

"Oh, okay." Nonie sounded disappointed. "Perhaps I shouldn't have been so keen for Max to leave, in that case."

"Well, can you try again to summon Barnabas? Don't forget you have a ferry to catch this evening."

Nonie nodded and closed her eyes. In a trice, her body froze. With her arms held tightly to her sides, her body rose upward and she transformed into Barnabas. She spoke in his voice.

"Why are you still here? Did you not heed the warnings?"

"We own Greenacres. We won't be leaving here," Greta replied, staring at the upright figure of Nonie. She looked like she was being suspended in thin air. Her feet were hardly touching the ground. She still clutched hold of her handbag.

"You must leave here, immediately! Before it is too late!" Barnabas dictated.

"No, I think you misunderstand us. You must leave, Barnabas. *You*, not us." Greta stood her ground.

"I cannot leave; I told you I am damned to stay here, forever."

"Well, I'm sorry but it's time for you to leave us; to leave this world. You are being given the chance to leave. You must look to the light. When you see it, you must follow it. Over the bridge, follow the light, Barnabas. You will find peace there. You are in the wrong place here. You have been stuck here for so long. You must be exhausted. For you to rest in peace, you must walk towards the light. Do you see it? Now go, follow it. It is your exit from this world. Take this opportunity. Go!"

Greta stood with bated breath. Nonie was still standing to attention with her arms at her sides. She was breathing erratically. Her eyes remained closed.

"Follow the light, Barnabas!" Greta repeated. "You will find peace there!"

There was silence. Nonie released her clutch on the handbag and it dropped to the floor. It startled Nonie, who opened her eyes. She held her forehead and blinked.

"Has he gone?" Greta whispered.

"Yes, I believe he has," Nonie replied.

Greta handed Nonie a glass of water. She took it and drank it straight down without breathing.

"Fantastic! He has actually gone," Greta sighed.

Nonie leant against the kitchen work surface. She rummaged around in her handbag and took out one of the pink pills and swallowed it without water. She made a face.

"Ergh! Okay, my job is done here. Barnabas has gone."

"Great. Right, well. I'll take you to the ferry terminal. You might just catch the 6 o'clock sailing from Ryde Pier Head. Ready?" Greta asked.

"I'm ready," Nonie smiled.

"Here. I think this should cover your expenses," Greta handed Nonie a folding of notes.

Nonie gratefully took the money without counting it and placed it in her handbag.

"He won't come back again, will he?" Greta needed reassurance.

"No, not now." Nonie spoke with a choked voice.

"Are you all right?"

"Yes, just exhausted, dear. It has been a bit hectic these last few days." Nonie gathered up her handbag, straightened her jacket and smiled up at Greta. "Let's hit the road."

They met Max driving down the track. Greta opened the window on the car and called out.

"All clear! Barnabas has gone. I'm taking Nonie back to the ferry."

"Oh right, good stuff. Thanks Nonie, nice to have made your acquaintance!" Max called from his car. "Safe journey back to England!"

"Goodbye, Max. Good luck!" Nonie responded.

"Thank you. But I don't need it!" Max waved.

"You might do," Nonie uttered under her breath.

Greta didn't take any notice of the exchange. They drove in silence to Ryde. Greta parked the car at the pier head, opened the boot and took out Nonie's luggage.

"Thanks for you help, Nonie." Greta kissed her on the cheek.

"You're welcome, my dear."

"You'll keep in touch?" Greta asked.

"Course I will, dear." Nonie smiled and took the case from Greta. "Ah good, the ferry's in. Goodbye!"

Greta watched the little figure walking along the gangplank and handing her ticket to the steward dressed in a fluorescent waistcoat. She got back into her car and watched as the vessel left the pier, smoke billowing from its vertical exhaust pipes as the engines burst into life.

"I sincerely hope I don't have to see you again," Greta thought to herself as the catamaran disappeared across the Solent.

❑❑❑

Max was in the kitchen at Greenacres when he heard a strange noise coming from the drawing room. He put down his half-eaten sandwich and decided to investigate. When he walked into the room, he couldn't see anything. He concluded it must have been the wind blowing against the windows. It was starting to get dark and the wind speed had strengthened considerably in the last half hour.

"Must be a storm brewing," he mumbled and walked back to the kitchen.

He hadn't noticed the small black figure running stealthily from the back door, through the kitchen and disappearing down into the well hole. The athletic figure deftly scaled the ladder and reached the passage floor in double quick time. Rolling onto its side and onto its feet, the figure resumed a crouched stance and looked around in a searching fashion.

Max put the kettle on and spooned coffee into a cup.

The figure drew out a knife and held it at arm's length. It inched its way along the passage, placing one foot slowly in front of the other, looking back as it made its way towards the wooden door.

Max added a spoonful of sugar.

The figure held the knife to the latch and levered the door open in silence. Dust fell sparingly from around the frame. The figure crept into the room and lit a match.

The kettle boiled and Max poured the boiling water into the cup.

Staring around the space, Ardi spotted the wooden box on the floor. She crouched in front of it and slowly lifted the lid. She gasped in awe at the gold, which shone back at her from inside the box. The match extinguished and Ardi reached for a pocket torch from inside her leather jacket. She shone the light onto the gold and thrust her hand through the layers. She smiled and nodded to herself.

"Thees is my ticket out of 'ere," she whispered and pulled a cloth bag from inside her jacket. She filled it until it brimmed with coins and jewels. She tied the bag with a piece of rope and pulled it hard so it knotted. She thrust a handful of coins inside her jacket pocket and zipped it up.

Max added a dash of long-lasting milk. He made a face.

"Ergh, give me real milk any time... what the...!" He heard another noise coming from the drawing room. He decided to reinvestigate, given Greenacres' past history of events and happenings. Walking back to the kitchen he was distracted by his mobile phone ringing in his trouser pocket. He stopped to answer it. Greta was on the end of the line.

"Hey! Have you got visitors?" she asked.

"No, not that I am aware of," Max replied. "Why?"

"Because I am driving down the track and there is a motorbike parked in the front yard," Greta replied.

"I haven't seen anyone. No one has knocked on the door."

"No matter. I'll be there in a tick, so I can find out who it is." Greta ended the call.

Max made a face and placed his phone back into his pocket. He walked towards the back door when he fell to the floor like a stone. Ardi, desperately trying to make her escape, had realised Max was in her way and stopped him in his tracks by hitting him over the head with the bag of gold. Not completely unconscious but dazed, he tried to scramble to his feet.

"Who the... hell are you?" he moaned, holding on to his neck. "Get out of my... ergh..."

Max sank to the floor in agony as he took another blow to the back of his head. He was knocked out cold. Ardi drew a hood over her head and zipped her jacket collar up to her face so she couldn't be identified. She grabbed

211

hold of the bag of gold and made for the door. She didn't expect to be disturbed by Greta, who was stood with her hand on the handle.

"Jesus! What are you doing?" Greta couldn't speak as the small hooded figure pushed her aside to the ground and sprinted for all she was worth to the waiting motorbike.

"Max! Max! Where are you?" Greta screamed. "Oh no!"

She found Max's lifeless body lying on the floor face down. She turned him over and checked for a pulse. He was alive. "Wake up! Wake up!" she yelled. "Come on, Max. Please! I need you!"

There was no response. Greta rushed outside and saw the figure mount the motorbike which sped off up the track. Greta took out her phone and pressed the camera facility. She snapped pictures of the motorbike and its riders as it disappeared out of view. At the end of the track, the motorbike came to an abrupt halt. It was as though it had hit an invisible barrier. Amazingly it turned tail and began driving back to the cottage. Greta continued to take photographs. It stopped and turned quickly away from her. The bike was on full throttle. The rider and passenger were shouting at the top of their voices. Greta couldn't decipher what they were saying. She decided to film the unexplainable happening on her phone's video recorder. What happened next made her gasp in horror.

The motorbike stalled and both people were thrown high into the air. Greta continued to film them. Their bodies hit the ground with an incredible force, one didn't move. The other had started to run towards Greta, screaming at the top of her voice. It was a small figure, dressed in black. Greta thought the voice had a familiar ring to it. She continued to film.

"Help! You must 'elp me! 'Elp!" the voice screamed.

Greta looked on in horror as the figure approached her. Ardi was only a matter of feet away when she was scooped up and hurled into the air, high above the trees into the nearby field. She screamed hysterically once more and was then silent. Greta continued to film as she climbed the fence and walked over to the figure lying in the grass. It didn't move.

Tentatively, Greta reached down and pulled the hood from the face of the person. She stepped back in shock as she revealed Ardi with blood pouring from her nose and mouth. She could also see that she was holding a cloth bag, which was losing some of its contents. She prised the bag from Ardi's grip to reveal a collection of gold.

Greta stood upright and bowed her head.

"How could you? You thieving little bitch!" She threw the bag to the floor in disgust.

"Greta!"

Greta turned to see Max staggering towards her, holding his head.

"Did you catch them? Did you?" he moaned.

"No, I didn't catch them; but something else did."

Greta pointed to the body.

"Look familiar to you, does she?"

Max tried to focus. "No, who is it?"

"Darling little brother's girlfriend... Ardi, no less!" Greta spat the name.

"You are joking! Surely not!" Max tried again to focus but his head was throbbing.

"The plot thickens, doesn't it? How on earth did she know about the gold? There has to be a major conspiracy going on here. But stupid little cow, it's cost her dearly; her life!"

"You mean... she's dead?"

"As a doornail, darling. And you should have seen the

way she left this world. It was spectacular. I have videoed it all. It will be great evidence for the police."

"So what exactly happened?" Max was still in shock.

"She, and her accomplice, who I don't know is still alive or not, were riding up the drive on the motorbike I saw earlier, when something stopped them dead. It was unbelievable. The bike appeared like it had a mind of its own. Then, whatever it was launched them both in the air, and pop! That was it, no more Ardi. Out like a light!"

"I don't think I can take much more of this," groaned Max. "Can you ring for help? Police, better get an ambulance too."

Greta dialled 999 and requested assistance.

As they waited for the emergency services, Greta was trying to make sense of what she had experienced. It was astonishing how the motorbike was kept from leaving Greenacres. An invisible force had prevented their escape. Greta needed to find out who or what was behind it.

Chapter Twenty-Seven

Greta was woken by a scratching sound near her head. The noise was coming from the bedstead. She opened her eyes and listened.

"Greta? Wake up!"

"Willow?" Greta mumbled.

"Yes."

"What happened today? Do you know?"

"Yes. He was furious; so very angry!"

"Who?"

"The man. He was furious that she stole the gold."

"You mean Barnabas?"

"Yes."

"Was it him that prevented the motorbike from leaving Greenacres?"

"Yes, he was so angry that the woman took his gold. He didn't want her to take it, so he stopped her."

"Wow, he certainly did. Where is he now?"

"He hasn't left; he is still here."

"Oh great, I thought we had got rid of him. What about Evie?"

"She is here too."

"So Nonie didn't succeed in moving him on to the next world, then?"

There was no reply.

"Willow?" Greta called into the darkness.

"Sadly, no," Willow eventually replied. "She doesn't see certain things; she is not capable of controlling the man. She is too weak, she isn't real; he will not leave until someone with more power is able to stand up to him."

"Great, what do you mean, she isn't real?" sighed Greta.

"She is not real. But I do know someone who is strong and courageous enough," Willow added.

"You do?" Greta sat up in bed, staring into the darkness. The alarm clock clicked to 2.30am.

"Yes. You," Willow replied.

"Me? You must be joking!"

"No, Greta. You are a very strong character. You are much stronger than the Reverend or the Nonie woman. You have the ability to deal with him. You must believe in yourself."

Greta looked puzzled.

"Willow? Willow?"

There was no reply. The bedroom resumed its silence. Greta lay back onto the bed and sighed. She thought about what Willow had suggested. Perhaps she might be the key in all of this; she hadn't really thought about her own ability as a medium. She closed her eyes and mulled it over in her mind until she drifted back to sleep. Max grunted in his sleep.

□□□

The next morning, Greta and Max met the police at Greenacres. They had cordoned off the lane with police tape as it remained a crime scene. The driver of the motorbike had survived and had been taken to hospital. He was in a critical condition with life-changing injuries and the police were extremely keen to question him.

Greta was taken to one side by an officer and asked to provide a statement. She duly obliged. Max also provided a statement. The police officer read through his notes.

"So did you know the person who had broken into your property, Mr Berkley?"

"Yes, it is… sorry, was, my brother-in-law's girlfriend, Ardi. She is, sorry was, from Poland. I'm sorry, I can't get my head around the fact that she's dead."

"That is fine, Mr Berkley. Do you know why she might want to break in to your property?"

"Yes, we, my wife and I, discovered some gold in a box, inside a tunnel in the kitchen. God, it sounds so far-fetched, doesn't it?" Max laughed as he spoke.

"If you don't mind, Mr Berkley, this is a very serious situation," the officer reminded Max.

"Sorry, of course, it is. Er, have they told Leo Standing about his girlfriend, yet?" Max tentatively asked.

"I don't know, sir. Can we continue, please?"

"Yes, of course." Max concentrated.

"Okay, right. This gold, the treasure, when did you discover it was in the, er… tunnel?" the officer glanced at his notes.

"Oh, only a couple of weeks ago. My wife was keen to leave it where it was. She is a bit of a psychic and felt it best to leave it be. I wasn't so sure. I thought it would be good to remove it."

"Even though this gold could well belong to the Crown?" The officer raised an eyebrow.

"Oh right, course. Hadn't thought of that." Max felt awkward.

"That will need to be established, Mr Berkley. Going

back to the deceased, how well did you know her?"

"Not that well. She always seemed to be with Leo, her boyfriend; she never said much. Seemed nervous, a twitchy sort of person. Wouldn't say boo to a ghost! Ha, sorry!" Max looked to the floor and bit his lip.

"Hmmm. How long have you owned the property, sir?"

"A few months, not that long. I can't really remember the date." Max looked puzzled. "What has that got to do with anything?"

"Just for our investigations. It was previously owned by a Reverend Oliphant, wasn't it?"

"Yes," Max agreed. "We bought Greenacres from him. He'd owned it for a long time."

"Did you see the property for sale in the local paper?"

"No, we… what does it matter?"

"Mr Berkley, if you don't mind," the officer continued.

"We, well, my wife, saw it from the pub window."

"Which pub, sir?"

"The Smuggler's Hide, up there." Max pointed to the hillside where the pub sat at the foot of the downs.

"So, who first noticed the cottage? Was your wife or Ms Nowak?"

"Um, well, I suppose it was Ardi, er, Ms Nowak. She was looking in the direction of it, admiring all the countryside, then casually pointed it out."

"Okay. What happened next?"

"What, at the pub?"

"Yes, if you don't mind, sir."

"Well, Greta saw the cottage and we went for a walk to have a look at it."

"We, sir?"

"Yes, Greta, Leo, Ardi and me."

"Ms Nowak went too?"

"Yes, she did. From what I remember, Leo was joshing Greta about the house being a, pardon my language, quote, *a shit hole*, for want of a better expression."

"And did Ms Nowak comment on its condition too?"

"No, she didn't get a chance as Greta was angry with Leo. He was tormenting her about the house being haunted. Greta pushed him and Ardi on to the grass. She was trying to brush her clothes down. The grass was quite wet, from what I remember. It was really funny!" Max recalled the incident with a smile.

"Is Mrs Berkley prone to explosive outbursts?"

"God, no! Greta wouldn't hurt a fly. Leo has this irritating habit of tormenting her. Stems from childhood, apparently. He pushes all the right buttons to upset her."

"Right. Thank you very much for the information, Mr Berkley. That's all for the moment."

"Don't you want to know about Ardi when she knocked me out with the bag of gold?"

"Uh, my colleague over there," the officer pointed to a man dressed in plain clothes, "would like to have a chat with you next, sir. Thank you for your time."

Greta was concentrating hard on her questions from the female officer.

"So you saw the motorbike when you drew into the lane?"

"Yes, there was a single beam light, in the yard. I knew it wasn't a car, unless it had a headlight out. Then I phoned Max to ask who was visiting him."

"What did he say?"

"That he didn't have visitors, then he was set upon by Ardi, she hit him on the back of the head with the bag. Knocked him out cold."

"Did you have a drink last night, Mrs Berkley?"

"No. I never drink and drive," Greta indignantly replied. "You can breathalyse me, if you want."

"Do you have witnesses who could confirm where you were last night?"

"Yes, I dropped Nonie off at the ferry terminal. She was the last person to see me before I drove home." Greta remembered Nonie staggering on to the catamaran at Ryde Pier.

"Nonie?" the officer replied.

"Yes, she had been visiting for the last few days." Greta nodded.

"Nonie who?"

"Spangler."

"Can you spell the name for me?" the officer was poised with her pen. Greta obliged.

"And what is your relationship with Nonie Spangler?"

"She is a celebrity medium." Greta felt embarrassed.

"And the reason for her visit?"

Greta groaned. "You're going to tell me, aren't you?"

"If you don't mind, Mrs Berkley, please." The officer jotted notes down on her pad without looking up.

"She was investigating a supernatural activity here," Greta spluttered. She felt her face redden.

"And did she discover any supernatural activity?"

Greta cringed.

"Yes."

"Mrs Berkley, how long have you know Ms Spangler?"

"As I said before, a few days, a couple of weeks at the most."

"So you aren't aware that she is not a spiritual medium, then?" the officer announced and looked directly at Greta.

"No! Why? What are you suggesting?"

"My colleagues in London have made me aware earlier this week, that the so-called celebrity medium named Nonie Spangler, is in fact wanted by them for a string of fraudulent offences, namely for conning people out of money with her claims to be a medium. She has been on the run for the last few weeks. They have informed me that she has been staying with you and your parents here on the Island."

Greta was horrified.

"I can't take all this in. You are saying she is a fake?"

"Allegedly, yes."

Greta looked alarmed.

"You aren't suggesting we were harbouring her from the police, are you?"

"This is what we need to establish, Mrs Berkley," the officer continued and looked at her notes.

Greta was stunned. She felt sick as she thought about the money she had given to Nonie, the fact that she had arranged for her to be a guest in her parents' house and the pure insolence and gall for posing as a medium. She thought about her argument with her father and shook her head in shame. She swallowed and distantly listened to the officer's continual questioning.

"You have told me about the motorbike and the accident, haven't you?"

"Ummm? Oh, yes, sorry. You can have a look at the footage on my phone, I videoed it. It's all on here," Greta pointed to her phone.

"We will need your phone as evidence. Can you please hand it over?" the officer asked.

"No, sorry, I can't. Someone might ring me; I can't possibly let you have the phone."

"Mrs Berkley. There is vital evidence on your mobile phone. I am sorry, but I must insist." The officer held out a plastic evidence bag and indicated for Greta to drop it in.

Greta was incensed. She threw the phone angrily into the bag. The officer swiftly sealed it and handed to one of her colleagues.

"I need it back as soon as you are finished with it!" she hissed.

"All in good time, Mrs Berkley."

"I don't feel like the victim here. I feel like the accused!" Greta retorted.

"It is all procedure, Mrs Berkley. You have witnessed a very serious crime. Not a very pleasant one in that. I understand that you are upset." The officer tried to reassure Greta.

"This is not a dream anymore."

"Mrs Berkley?" The officer looked puzzled.

"It's all a bloody nightmare! It was supposed to be our dream; our dream cottage in the countryside. Escaping the rat race, coming back home to live in peace on the Island. Instead it is turning into an episode in our lives I don't want to be part of anymore." Greta gulped back a tear.

"How well did you know Ms Nowak?"

"Ardi? A bit. She was quiet, in Leo's shadow most of the time."

"So she didn't appear manipulative then?"

"Not at all."

"Would you say she was capable of committing a crime?"

"No, she didn't seem strong or clever enough."

"We have managed to obtain a little bit of background information on Ms Nowak," the officer continued. "How long had she been seeing your brother?"

"Oh, must be six months or so." Greta pushed her hair away from her eyes. She glanced over at Max who was sitting on the stone garden seat. He looked very pale.

"Did Ms Nowak have a job here?"

"Yes, she was working at one of the local salad growers' farms."

"Was it a permanent position?"

"I don't know. She never spoke about her work."

"Would it surprise you to know that she had in fact lost her job?"

"Yes! I had no idea." Greta looked shocked. "She never mentioned it."

"We have discovered that she was sacked as she was caught stealing from her employer. A couple of months ago."

Greta sighed. She thought of Leo.

"Does my brother know about this?"

"An officer is with him as we speak. So he will be aware of Ms Nowak's demise."

"But does he know about her thieving?"

"I don't know, Mrs Berkley."

Greta looked over to Max again. He had his head in his hands.

"That will be all for the time being. Thank you for your cooperation, Mrs Berkley." The officer glanced at her watch. "We might need to question you further down at the station, but I will be in contact with you, if we do." She handed Greta her business card.

"Well, don't bother ringing me on my mobile." Greta looked at the card sulkily. "You had better take my parents' home number."

Greta walked over to Max. He looked up at her and managed to smile.

"It all happens here on the beautiful Garden Isle, doesn't it?" he croaked. "My head and neck still ache; bloody Ardi. Can you believe she's dead, love? I certainly can't. I wonder how Leo is feeling?"

"Pretty gutted, I can imagine. By the way, the police have taken my phone as evidence, so don't ring me for the time being." Greta sat down beside Max and held on to his arm.

"How did Ardi know about the gold?" Max shook his head.

"It was Leo, of course. He was down in the tunnel, wasn't he? I bet he was trying to steal the gold. When he tried to climb down, he must have fallen, hence the broken ankle. Oh, and did you know that Ardi had been sacked from her job?"

"No!" Max looked stunned. "How? Why?"

"For stealing!" Greta looked angrily up at the roof of Greenacres.

"Bloody hell! So she was short of dosh and decided to cash in on our stash of booty then?"

"Yep, conniving little cow! Still, she won't be stealing any more, will she?"

"But if that was the case, how did Leo know about it?"

"Think about it, Max. I know I am gullible, but I think I might have the reason." Greta looked smug.

"Go on," Max prompted.

"Remember how anxious the Rev Oli always was when you mentioned the demise of his tenant?"

"Yes."

"And the reason he gave for his anxiety, just before he died?"

"Yes."

"Well, there is your answer."

Max thought for a while.

"You mean, Marcus Mowbrie?"

"The same. He had a hold over Rev Oli, didn't he? Insisted that the Rev was to sell Greenacres to him and no one else. Mowbrie must have known about the gold."

"Yes, old news."

"So who do you think would be in a position to assist Marcus Mowbrie?"

"Leo and Ardi?"

"Yep, Laurel and Hardy. She was out of work, out of money. Leo's work doesn't pay that well. They were short of cash. Also, there is something interesting the police mentioned earlier. When they asked how long Leo and she had been together, I said about six months. Six months... six months before a work permit runs out? Coincidence, don't you think?"

"Possibly. I thought it didn't matter about permits now. Anyway... and?"

"Mowbrie was in the pub that time when we had the family lunch, wasn't he?"

"Yes."

"He interrupted our conversation, overheard us when we talked about Greenacres."

"He did."

"Don't you think it was coincidence that he was on the table next to ours and was in earshot?"

"Hadn't really thought about it." Max scratched his head. "Have you mentioned all this to the police?"

"Not yet, but I think I am about to. Oh and they have inside information on Nonie too, sadly it's not good news."

Max shook his head.

"She is a fake, isn't she?"

Greta kissed Max on the cheek.

"Yes, she is wanted by the Met for fraud and she's been on the run for a fortnight. Sorry, Max, you were right. So was the father. The police want to ask me some more questions. I think I need to go to the station with them. They want more information on Nonie."

Max looked alarmed.

"You aren't being arrested, are you?" he called back to Greta, who was being escorted by an officer to a waiting car.

"No, don't be silly. They just want to ask a few questions. Wish me luck!"

Chapter Twenty-Eight

"Let me get this straight, Mrs Berkley. You have said you attended a show in London with Ms Spangler as the star act."

"Yes, she was carrying out a spiritual evening. It was one of her nights on tour."

"Trouble is, she wasn't on a nationwide tour. That night you attended was the only night she was booked to perform."

Greta looked baffled.

"But her website… the newspaper said she was on tour…" she broke off and put her hand to her mouth.

"One of her wheezes, unfortunately. I did tell you she is a con artist. Right, then you employed her to investigate… uh… what did you say…?"

Greta looked humiliated.

"Paranormal activity…" she whispered.

"At your newly acquired property?"

"Yes." Greta ran her hand through her hair.

"Didn't it seem odd to you that she was able to come over to the Island on a whim to your property? If she was on a nationwide tour, she wouldn't have been able to drop everything, she would have had pre-arranged show dates. Don't you find that odd, Mrs Berkley?"

Greta shook her head.

"No. Because I thought she was… oh… genuine."

"That's how confidence tricksters operate, Mrs Berkley. They win your trust; get you to like them, to trust them. That's how it works. Sadly this is not the first time I have investigated this sort of crime and, no doubt, it won't be the last."

"Right," Greta answered bleakly. She wished Max were with her.

"So, she found paranormal activity in the cottage?"

"So she said; but then, so did I."

"How did she deal with it?"

Greta thought back to Nonie's first visit.

"She wasn't much help."

"Did you pay her at this stage?"

"Yes, I paid her and gave her money for her travelling expenses."

"Did she solve your paranormal problem on that occasion?"

Greta felt terrible.

"No. She told me she was sapped of energy."

"Didn't that ring any alarm bells to you? At this stage, Mrs Berkley?"

"No, because I thought… she was genuine." Greta closed her eyes in humiliation.

"But then, you called her back on another occasion." The officer continued to barrage Greta with questions.

Greta looked to the ceiling.

"Yes," she whispered.

"And did she solve your paranormal problem?"

"Sort of; but then… well, no."

"Did you pay her on that occasion?"

"No, I offered her to stay over at my parents' property as she was feeling drained and weak; she suffers from asthma. I took pity on her. She stayed at their property."

"Was she alone at the property for any length of time?"

"She was in her room, on the first afternoon, resting," Greta recalled.

"Was there any other time she was alone at your parents' property?"

Greta thought hard.

"Hmmn, not that I remember."

"Have your parents reported anything missing from their property?"

Greta shook her head.

"No, mummy hasn't said anything has gone missing."

The officer scribbled further notes on a pad.

"I think we need to make them aware of Ms Spangler's situation. And we need them to check for any missing items."

"It's all been rather hectic, with my brother in hospital; I haven't had a chance to speak with them yet. They are very upset about Leo, no doubt they will be devastated about Ardi; they really thought a lot of her," Greta surmised.

"Okay, thank you very much for the information you have given us this afternoon. We will be in touch if we need to speak to you any more." The officer closed her notebook and indicated towards the door.

"You will let me know what happens in respect of Nonie, won't you?" Greta looked over to the officer as she made her way to the door.

"Of course," was the swift reply. "Goodbye, Mrs Berkley."

"Bye." Greta closed the door behind her.

To her surprise, Max was in the reception area. He looked very worried and rushed over to Greta's side.

"Darling, are you all right?" He held her close to his chest.

"Yes, I'm fine. I'm free to go, don't worry, Max." She squeezed him back. They walked out of the police station and over to where Max had parked the car.

"All this just doesn't seem real," Greta reflected, she drifted into a daydream. "It all just seems like a crazy dream…"

□□□

"Greta! Greta? Darling, can you hear me?"

Greta frowned.

"Now what? Yes, I can hear you, mummy."

"Oh thank goodness. You really had us all really very worried," her mother's voice permeated the air.

Greta blinked. For some reason her eyes were closed but she could quite clearly hear her mother's voice.

"Mummy? What's wrong?" She opened her eyes and focused on Jeanne who was standing over her. Her face was white.

"Darling, do you know where you are?"

Greta thought her mother had been on the sherry.

"Of course I know where I am. Max and I have just left the police station…" she blinked her eyes once again. "Why are you dressed up like that? You look really smart! What's he doing here?" She was staring at the paramedic.

Her mother smiled. She looked relieved.

"Because it's your wedding day. How are you feeling?"

"But I'm already married. We got married ages ago…" Greta stopped talking, paused and looked down at what she was wearing. She felt constricted in her clothes.

"Why… mummy, what's going on?" Greta was confused.

"You had a bit of a fright, darling. In fact, you had a terrible fright…" her mother began.

"Well, we all have, haven't we? What with everything that happened at Greenacres, Ardi, Leo and Barnabas."

Her mother looked surprised.

"What is Greenacres, darling?"

"Mummy, have you got amnesia? You know, *Greenacres!*"

"Sorry, darling, you've lost me. Maxim, do you want to speak to Greta?" Jeanne looked alarmed. "I think she is still concussed," she added in a whisper.

Max knelt beside Greta and took her hand.

"Greta, it's Max, darling."

"Oh, thank the lord, please talk some sense to me." Greta was relieved to see Max.

Max smiled nervously.

"Your mother is right, darling. It *is* our wedding day. You had an unfortunate encounter with a spider; fainted and fell. When you fell you hit your head on the edge of the table. You've been out stone cold for quite a long while."

Greta looked annoyed.

"Don't be so silly. Don't you remember where we've been and what's been happening?"

"No, I have been with you, here at the hotel all the time. I haven't been anywhere and neither have you." Max held Greta's hand. "We did complete the ceremony, before you blacked out. But the minister had to leave. She had another wedding to attend. We will have to rearrange another time to collect the marriage certificate; she said it would be all right. We'll have to wait until you are feeling better." Max looked bleakly at Greta.

Greta smiled.

"Ha, ha! I'm really not that gullible, Max, but nice try." She laughed and waited for Max's response.

"Seriously, without a word of a lie. You fainted; it's still our wedding day. That knock on the head must have really had an impact on your memory. Don't worry, we are legally married."

Greta looked down at her clothes and blinked in astonishment. She was wearing her wedding gown. Her posy of limp roses lay on the floor and her parents were stood either side, trying to force disappointed smiles.

The paramedic was packing up his equipment.

"Greta will be fine. I am leaving now, but ring again if there are any problems."

"Thank you very much." Max shook the paramedic's hand.

"Well done, old girl. Nice to see you back with us; in the land of the living!" Charles stepped forward. His foot crushed the bouquet of roses. Jeanne yelled at the top of her voice.

"Charles! You stupid fool! Watch where you are treading! You must be more careful!" Jeanne knelt down and scooped up the flattened roses. She wailed in despair. "Just to add to all the drama!"

"Don't worry mummy; it's not the end of the world." Greta struggled to her feet from the floor. She brushed down her wedding gown and put a hand to her head. She felt her tiara. It was still safely in place. "Compared to what I have been through, this is a walk in the park!"

Jeanne held out her hand to steady Greta. Greta smiled.

"It's okay; I'm feeling much better. I could do with a drink, though." She looked at her bouquet. "I think we'll leave this in here; it's seen better days!"

Max held out his hand and Greta thankfully took it.

"Are you okay to carry on?" he asked.

"Of course, yes. I wouldn't miss this for the world. It has taken ages to plan. We must enjoy it. Come on, let's go and find the guests."

Max looked relieved.

"You must tell me some time about what you've been through. From what you were saying, it was something pretty memorable."

Greta stopped suddenly and looked in alarm at Max.

"Where's Leo?"

"He's here somewhere, in the garden, I think."

"Is he all right? How is his ankle?"

Max looked baffled.

"Yeah, he's fine, and so is his ankle."

"Good, I'm so glad."

"Really? Where did that come from?"

Greta frowned.

"Not sure. What about Ardi? Is, is she…"

"Yes, Ardi is here too."

Greta looked pale.

"Just one more thing." She held tightly on to Max's arm.

"Yes?"

"Who married us?"

Max smiled with uncertainty.

"Uh, it was a Miss, oh sorry, can't remember her name."

"So it was a female? Not a man?"

"No, originally it was going to be the vicar, Reverend Oliphant. But he was taken ill. She stepped in at the last minute for him."

Greta looked shocked. "But he is okay?"

"Yes, just some sort of virus. Nothing life threatening."

"Right."

"What difference does that make?" Max was intrigued.

Greta paused.

"No difference. I just wanted to make sure he was all right. Must be horrible being struck down."

"He's on the mend. Sends his very best regards to us both and he wishes us every happiness for the future, I think that's what the card read. I took a peek whilst you were... um... not in this world."

"Have you ever heard of someone called Marcus Mowbrie?" Greta continued to rack Max's brain.

"Marcus... no, can't say I have."

"That's good; I don't want you know him. He's not a good person."

"You obviously know him, by all accounts," Max surmised.

"Not really, just an acquaintance. No, perhaps not even that."

"Did I hear you mention Marcus Mowbrie?" Leo was stood in front of Greta.

"Oh Leo! You are okay! Thank god!" Greta threw herself into Leo's arms, much to his surprise. He managed to untangle Greta's vice-like grip on him. He held her at arm's length.

"Bloody hell! You must have taken a real hard knock to your brain, sis." He laughed.

"Are you all right with me?" Greta looked seriously at Leo.

He stopped laughing.

"Of course I am, what makes you think otherwise?"

"So you're not jealous then?"

Leo thought hard for a moment.

"Er, no. Can't say I am. You're my sister, how could I be jealous of you?"

Greta hugged him tightly.

"I'm so glad; you will never know how much," she whispered close to his ear.

"I think you need a lie down, Greta. You've gone all mushy! Oh, and why did you want to know about Marcus Mowbrie?"

Greta held Leo away from her.

"Do you know him?" she asked.

"Yes, sort of. He's a local farmer. Has a farm not that far from mum and dad's place. You've known of him for years as well."

Greta looked puzzled.

"Have I? Where does he live?"

Leo grinned.

"Near Greenacres Farm. I heard he's been trying to buy the place recently. Bit of a struggle from all accounts. The place is a real wreck apparently. It's owned by the local vicar, so I've been told."

Greta looked alarmed. "How do you know all this?"

Leo looked sheepish.

"Sorry, perhaps I've said too much. It needs renovating. Why, what's wrong with that?"

"Does he know about its past, the history?" Greta looked around her in desperation.

"Haven't got a clue," Leo replied. "I should imagine he's aware of it though. Apparently he has some sort of connection with it. Something to do with his family, some years ago. How come you know all about it? It's not one of your supernatural projects, is it? I didn't know you dabbled that much into the unknown!"

"Hmmm, he should be careful. Be really careful. I wonder if he knows about the tunnel! I wonder if he's come across Barnabas!"

Max and Leo looked baffled.

"Do you think she is all right? The bump on her head seems to have made her talk a lot of gibberish," Leo whispered.

"Leo, do you know something more about Greenacres than you are letting on?"

Leo frowned. "Can't say, sis. Too much information…"

Greta walked away from Leo and took Max's hand.

Taking a deep breath, Greta shrugged her shoulders and marched forward.

"What is wrong with Leo, Max? He is acting really weird."

Max smiled and took hold of Greta's hand.

"I shouldn't worry about Leo. But I do have a little wedding gift for you. It is supposed to be a surprise, but, seeing as you've had a bit of a rough start to our married life, I…"

Greta interrupted him and pointed to the table. "What's that?"

Max smiled.

"Oh, I nearly forgot; Reverend Oliphant has left a gift. It was delivered by the minister. It's over there. On the card he has written that it *is a little memento of our special day.* Sent with his apologies that he couldn't attend."

Max led Greta over towards the table where a large gift-wrapped box had been placed along with the card. She took hold of the box and ripped the paper aside. Inside was a wooden box. She lifted the lid and gasped in amazement. She steadied herself as she felt her legs buckle from beneath her.

"Oh god, Max! It's the gold!" she shrieked. "It's the gold!"

"Gold? Wow, really? Hey, you don't seem very surprised. You're behaving like you already knew about it. We must thank him straight away. Is it real?"

Greta ran her fingers over gold coins and trinkets and smiled in satisfaction, for the sake of her sanity.

"Oh yes, it certainly is for real. It's most definitely for real! It isn't a dream!"

"Then you had better take this too." Max handed Greta a small green box.

Greta took the box and lifted the lid. Her jaw dropped

and she looked at him in disbelief. Inside was an old key laying on a green velvet pad. She gasped.

Max smiled.

"To my beautiful wife, the key to my heart! No, seriously, it's the key to your dream cottage!"

Greta gulped and felt faint. Her nightmare was about to begin!